Dawson Junior G3
Brian Wagstaff

NORÐIC PRESS

Second Edition
Published by
Nordic Press
Kindlyckevägen 13
Rimforsa, Sweden.
2022

This is a work of fiction.
Similarities to real people, places, or
events are entirely coincidental.

DAWSON JUNIOR G3
9789198671049
Written by Brian Wagstaff
Cover Design by Derek Power
Formatting by
Christopher Clawson Rule
With additional work by C. Marry Hultman

Acknowledgments

In completing this book I owe a great debt of gratitude to large numbers of people.

First I would like to mention Jane Willis, Paddy Mahony, and Bernhard and Ellen Bug, who read the manuscript of Dawson Junior G3 and gave feedback, offering criticisms and comments, and suggesting corrections. Their remarks helped me to give a sharper focus to the story and to strengthen the coherence of the plot and themes, not to mention enabling me to eliminate some embarrassingly poorly-worded sentences where my concentration had obviously slipped while writing. Of course it goes without saying that any faults in this novella are my own, not due to them.

Jane and Paddy were both classmates of mine in the MA course in Creative Writing at Anglia Ruskin University, which greatly helped me to develop my writing skills. The general university ethos and spirit of enquiry which prevailed in the classes was enormously helpful, but I would like to single out two tutors for special mention.

Caron Freeborn (1966 – 2020) ran the novel workshop module which I attended in 2014. She was lively, funny, and unfailingly supportive. She taught me a great deal, especially about the subtler aspects of narrative point of view. Her sudden death, from cancer, in spring this year, was a terrible shock to all who knew her. To repeat the words of her friend, the historical novelist Elizabeth Speller, 'Rest in (not too much) peace, Caron!' Those who know Caron would get the joke – too much peace would be boring! And thank you, Caron, for so much encouragement and time gladly given!

Una McCormack ran the Patterns of Story module and was also my supervisor on my Major Project in 2016. Apart from being a very fine science fiction writer, she is an inspiring teacher who easily communicates her own enthusiasm for writing and especially for speculative fiction. For someone with my tastes in writing, she was the obvious choice of supervisor.

One other huge influence must be mentioned (one for whom Una and I shared an enthusiasm) – Ursula le Guin, to my mind the finest of science fiction writers, at least of the ones I know. More than most SF writers she preferred not to dazzle the reader with science and technology for its own sake, but to focus on their effect on society. I hope this novella reflects the same emphasis.

I would also like to thank Patty McCarthy, Editor of Magazines at Breaking Rules Publishing. Her job is far from easy, but she has always been kind and enthusiastic in her dealings with me, and generous with her time. She has given me great encouragement, publishing many of my stories in The Scribe – a great magazine, you should read it! Knowing there is an editor out there who appreciates my work in a harsh world makes life so much easier.

Great thanks too to Christopher Clawson-Rule, the President and Founder of Breaking Rules Publishing, for having the confidence in me to publish this novella.

Lastly, thanks to you, reader, for buying this little book. I hope you enjoy it!

Wag, September 2020

Dedication

Paddy Mahony (1953 – 2020)

I mentioned Paddy in the Acknowledgments as one of the readers who checked the manuscript of this novella in advance. He sent his comments to me – typically acute, quirky, effusive, generous, good-humoured and full of high spirits (and obscenity!) – by email towards the end of June 2020. Sadly, he was unexpectedly taken ill just over a month later, and passed away at the beginning of the following September.

I had known him for twenty years or more, first as a teaching colleague at The Cambridge Academy of English, then as a friend, who lived round the corner from me, and finally as a classmate and fellow writer. We frequently compared thoughts on literature, writing, and human values over rather too many glasses of Irish whisky. He was an excellent writer – one of the stars in our year of the Anglia Ruskin MA in Creative Writing.

More than most of us, Paddy knew how to celebrate, mourn, and express what it is to be human, and this little book is dedicated to his memory.

Rest in Peace, Paddy!

DAWSON JUNIOR G3

The Door of number 81 Oak Avenue flashed all its red lights and sounded its hazard guidance repeatedly:

'WARNING: POTENTIAL THREAT. DO NOT APPROACH DOOR UNTIL LIGHTS STOP FLASHING. DO NOT PROCEED BEYOND GATE. WARNING…'

All owners of Doors were obliged by law to have gates far enough away to ensure the safety of innocent passers-by in the event of an explosion or other mishap during a Door Encounter.

The drone whose proximity had triggered the warning hung, busily whirring, as it initiated the greeting protocol and waited for a response. The Door analysed the drone's electronic bona fides giving the origin of its journey, the purpose of its visit, and its protestation of peaceful intent (PPI). The PPI was a standard electronic form which stated that the drone bore no weapons or other threats and no illegal products.

Cautiously satisfied that the bona fides were in order, the Door slid down a protective cover, allowing a slot to appear through which a large shelf emerged. The drone came to rest on this, cutting its engines. Clasps extended from the surrounds of the Door to hold the drone captive until the transaction was completed. Simultaneously, on both sides of the Doorframe a battery of sensors, probes and weapons emerged, pointing at the drone, in case the PPI turned out to be false. These analysed the composition of the drone itself and inspected the contents of its package in detail to ensure that it contained no explosives, poisons or other toxic substances such as narcotics, and nothing illegal. A dedicated computer stood ready to activate whatever equipment was needed to neutralise any threat. If necessary, the package and/or the drone itself would be destroyed. The means of doing so included, among a range of other options, controlled explosion, disassembly, the defusing of any bomb, or soaking with water. If a dangerous chemical were detected, or perhaps two or more elements which might be automatically mixed to create a poisonous gas, the substance would be instantaneously neutralised by the addition of whatever chemical the computer deemed necessary, of which a vast store was held ready. Any crime detected could be reported electronically, though this was dependent on permission from the Door owner: the early days of Door development had seen too many trivial incidents reported for the system yet to be trusted on this without guidance.

But on this occasion the transaction was revealed to be as innocent as the drone claimed.

The clasps relaxed and retreated into the Door's surrounds, the drone started its engines and whirred off, leaving its cargo behind, and the multitude of sensors, probes and weapons retracted. Then a large flap in the Door behind the shelf opened inwards, the shelf withdrew bearing its package, the flap closed again and locked, and the slot's cover hummed up to its former protective position.

And the whole system was put on standby for the next potential threat.

Frank, sitting upstairs in his study working on the latest entry to his on-line column, became aware of the arrival of a package when he heard

'CAUTION: POTENTIAL THREAT. DO NOT PROCEED BEYOND ALCOVE DOOR UNTIL GREEN LIGHT SHOWS. CAUTION...'

In practice, Doors could eliminate any threat within very close confines, but legislation nevertheless imposed unnecessarily large safety zones both outside and inside the Door. In addition to the needlessly extensive area between the Door and the gate, the Door owner had to have a cavernous and heavily reinforced strong room (euphemistically named the Alcove) inside the Door, where the danger was negligible. It was the inner door of this Alcove which displayed the red or green lights according to threat levels. As a further safety measure, the inner Alcove door automatically locked when the lights were red. There was an override switch for the system of course, carefully protected and pass-worded, but who wants to override protection?

Shortly afterwards, Frank heard the further advisory:

'ALCOVE DOOR UNLOCKED. PACKAGE SAFE TO OPEN. CONTAINS FRAGRANT ALCOHOLIC LIQUID DEEMED HARM-LESS UNLESS IMBIBED. APPLY EXTER-NALLY AND DO NOT DRINK. REPEAT, DO NOT DRINK.'

Ten years ago, on hearing a package fall onto his Welcome mat, Frank might have run downstairs eager to discover what goodie await-ed him, but that was before he had acquired a Door – Dawson Junior ®™ G3 to give it its exact name. Now his lack of enthusiasm was obvious as he went into the Alcove and unwrapped the bottle of after-shave which his Aunt Lucy had sent. It was his 39th birthday, so the arrival of a present was no surprise.

He wondered if the Door had something to do with his recent low moods.

He went upstairs to his study and sat down at his computer. The busy sound of drones filled the air, and they created fleeting shadows as they blocked the sun briefly.

The message popped up on his screen 'They are amongst us.' He clicked his tongue and dismissed it, muttering 'fundamentalist nutters.' Then he entered the following thoughts into the computer:

We spend so much time and money buying equipment like the Door that will ensure our security. It's as if we equate safety with happiness. True, we can't be happy if we're dead. But doesn't it make us miserable constantly dwelling on the risks we're trying to avert? To me, life seemed more joyful when we were less safe. We felt much more alive then!

Frank published the comment, then with a smile he leaned back and waited for his readers' reactions. The first one was not long in coming.

Oh, so *YOU* felt more alive before the Door? And *WE* must all risk our own lives to stop *YOU* from feeling board!!! Selfish liberals like u make me sick. It's lucky we live in a democrasy so puffed up would be dictators like u can't make dangerous decisions for the rest of us. It's a dangerous world, mister Love and Peace! I'd like to go on living thanks very much, if that's ok with u!!!

Many more comments in the same vein followed in quick succession. Frank felt a quiet glow of satisfaction: such remarks were gold to him. The salary the state paid him as an on-line columnist and 'opinion-former' was greatly increased if he got comments or even reaction-emojis on his material, so it paid to be controversial. Not that he had any economic need to work. Like everyone else, he received a salary from the state which covered his needs adequately. Computers controlled the economy, and robots were responsible for all the industrial output, so there were few jobs for humans outside the advertising and marketing sector (by far the largest employer), the ethics panel's which were obligatory for every company, and politics. In addition, Frank had inherited money from his parents, who had died nine years ago. But he liked working on his column, and the state liked people to be purposefully occupied, which was why the government was happy to pay him for his work.

There was a loud clang, and the room went dark. The window shield had shot into its closed position. Doubtless one of the drones had got closer than the Door system deemed safe. The Door computer would be interrogating the drone, and the weapons around the window would have emerged from the window frame ready to strike, and would be tracking it until it was a safe distance away. The system would not allow any unauthorised person or object to come too close to an entry point. After a moment the shield moved back to its open position. This normally happened several times a day, yet Frank had never heard of a genuine attack.

He resumed his work:

And the amount of weaponry our houses display seems out of all proportion to the threat. Even at the time the Door was introduced, crime against people able to afford it was at historically low levels. Now it is almost non-existent. Yet we continue to behave as if we are in a state of war. Is this really necessary?

Once more, reactions arrived quickly. This

was the first:

Oh yeah? But I bet *YOU'VE* got a Door, haven't you? If it's so unnecessary, why have *you* got one? Forewarned is forearmed. It's only sensible to protect yourself and your property! That's what keeps crime low. If you've got a Door you're a hypocrite! And if you haven't you're an idiot! Hypocrite or idiot, which is it?

It was a fair question, though he had no intention of answering it. To do so truthfully would involve giving away information he regarded as unduly personal. He glanced at the framed photo of his parents, on his desk. When they heard of a revolutionary new system of home protection from HomeFortressCo, which armed every door and window in the house and could pulverise any intruder, they had made him promise to get one. They were very anxious people, and he was an only child: it would have been cruel to refuse. Then, once you had a Door, you got sucked into the whole industry of upgrading it regularly; not to do so seemed a waste of the initial investment, which was a considerable outlay.

The first version was called Dawe, a rather heavy pun, aimed at personifying the entrance to a house. The upgrade to that, son of Dawe as it were, was called Dawson. This was marketed as being like your own personal butler, footman and minder, all in one. It was a popular, reassuring concept with the public. Then there was Dawson Junior. After that the company ran out of naming ideas, so the next upgrades were Dawson Junior G 2 and then 3, which was Frank's version. The G stood for Generation, not that anyone paid much notice to the naming logic by this time: people just referred to 'the Door', and the initial letter was always capitalised.

Ironically, not long after he had acceded to their request his parents had died in a boating accident. They had always loved the sea, its wildness and unpredictability, and had left the harbour defying the weather warnings. The waves had spat their mangled bodies up on the rocks two days later, along with their wrecked vessel. Those most aware of danger, particularly to loved ones, were often most addicted to risk themselves. Frank knew that the agony of identifying their remains would haunt him for the rest of his life.

Early development of the Door was not

without controversy. Intrigued by this inno-
vation, and wondering what would happen, a
group of children threw stones at one of the
first examples, and were immediately killed by
the barrage of fire that followed. Predictably,
there was an uproar in the liberal media. The
manufacturers issued their deepest condolenc-
es to parents and relatives, but pronounced that
the deaths were 'a regrettable necessity.' However, HomeFortressCo prided itself on its con-
science and sense of responsibility to society,
and when a narrow majority of its Ethics Com-
mittee argued that the response of the system in
this case had been disproportionate, the company showed their good will by supplementing
the system's weapons with a taser and tear gas
to be used in cases like this in future to prevent
needless loss of life. But in any case, publicity
of the incident ensured that such an attack was
never repeated. Although HomeFortressCo
might have suffered damage to their reputation
in some quarters, sales of the Door rocketed after this, to such an extent that it was difficult to
meet demand.

It was also at this stage that the ruling Trad
Party Government took a stake in the compa-

ny, with the right to oversee regulations. They made a great show of their involvement, repeating their slogan, 'The Right To Sleep Safe In Your Bed', and were rewarded with an 8% jump in their already high approval ratings. The opposition Mod Party, whose manifesto promised to increase the involvement of AI in the economy and decrease human employment and intervention, offered little resistance to the measure except to urge scrapping the overseeing of regulations and unfettering the machines' decision-making.

'They are amongst us!' There was that annoying message on screen again. Frank wasn't the only recipient; all his acquaintances – three, no, five other people – got them as well. He had read about 'computer viruses' in history books. They had long been eliminated. Yet some similar phenomenon seemed to have invaded the computer system of his own time. No-one that Frank knew had any idea of the purposes of these messages. Were they warnings? Advertisements of some kind? Strangely, the Government information channels made no mention of this. Was it possible that this was beyond the power of the Government to control? Once more he dismissed the message.

Enough work for the morning, Frank thought. He called, 'Bella, Donna!'

'Coming, Frank!' chorused two young female voices, one with the trace of an Italian accent, the other a Japanese one. They entered the room a moment later, Bella slightly in the lead. Her skin was tanned and she had honey-blonde hair. She was dressed with classical simplicity. A short flap, suspended from a cord, hung loose over her breasts, while two even shorter flaps, hanging from a string round her waist, just covered her loins fore and aft. Quick-release knots on the right-hand side of both garments ensured that they could be removed with a minimum of effort. Donna was a little shorter than Bella, and was oriental in appearance. She was dressed the same as Bella, although the colour of the garments was different. Bella wore yellow flaps which went beautifully with her tan, and Donna wore red. Both of them had exceptionally beautiful figures and features. Neither wore underwear – they had no need for it, after all. Frank smiled: this would help to cheer him up.

Frank was well-off, and though not extravagant generally, he believed in enhancing his life with the luxuries that would make a real difference. So when it came to a choice of Companion, he had bought the finest money could buy – and not just one but two. It required sophisticated bio-mechatronic and genetic engineering to manufacture Companions, and it was an expensive process. It was rare for anyone to own more than one Companion, and many made do with hiring the unconvincing and obviously plastic versions available from the rental shops from time to time. Bella and Donna, in contrast, could not be distinguished from the real thing by any of the five senses. Only the tiny hollow at the base of their throats revealed that they were in fact machines. This was the socket into which their solar cloaks were plugged when they went 'sunbathing' on the patio outside to recharge.

'You are ready for lunch, Frank?' asked Bella. Her accent imposed a tiny extra syllable on his name – 'Franker'. She could speak flawless English, of course, as could Donna, but Frank found Italian and Japanese accents sexy, and had paid extra for them, so both Companions occasionally inserted inaccuracies in pronunciation typical of their supposed origins into their speech to keep him happy.

'We could make you an omelette – omelette' – Donna corrected herself, 'or you could have sushi, or chicken risotto with peas and broccoli. All of them are fine for your health needs right now.'

'Omelette would be great,' said Frank, 'but how about a spot of stress relief first, ladies?'

'Are you feeling tense, *caro*?' asked Bella, unbuttoning his shirt and stroking his chest softly. She kissed him on the lips.

'You work too hard. You know we always tell you that!' said Donna. She was paying attention to the lower half of Frank's body, with slow sensual caresses, bestowing a trail of moist kisses lower and lower on his stomach, while getting her hands gently inside his trousers.

Frank felt his cares melt away.

'Which one of us do you want?' whispered Donna.

'Or maybe you would like a threesome?' murmured Bella.

'Threesome,' Frank managed to say, almost overpowered by bliss.

***

Next day Frank's work was again interrupted by a Door Announcement.

'ALCOVE DOOR UNLOCKED. PACKAGE SAFE TO OPEN. CONTAINS INVITATION ON CARD IN GOLD EMBOSSED LETTERS. STRONGLY RECOMMEND ACCEPTANCE. REPEAT, **STRONGLY** RECOMMEND ACCEPTANCE.'

Frank groaned. Invitations were seldom good news, especially those on card and delivered by drone. This retro fashion was a way of flattering the recipients, an attempt to make them feel special, rather than just sending an email. The events were almost always organised and paid for by government and aimed at getting people socialising with one another. His need for company was already supplied by Bella and Donna. He did get conversation, of a kind, with other humans via comments on his on-line column – and his estimate of their intelligence was not very high.

'But Flank, you need company of your own kind,' said Donna.

'Yes, she is right,' said Bella. 'Don't be a – *come se dice,* how you say? – stick in the mudder, Frank. It will be fun.'

Frank doubted that very much. But he knew that, though worded as an invitation, this was not far from an order. Not attending could entail a substantial fine, or his taxes might rise drastically, or, worst of all, he could be forbidden to work on his column. And even if none of these things happened, Bella and Donna would nag him endlessly. All Companions were programmed to spread government propaganda.

'And think of the girls that will be there!' said Bella.

That was the real reason for the invitation, of course. The population had been plummeting for almost two centuries, and the state was desperate to arrest and eventually reverse the decline.

'Oh, all right!' he said.

***

'I will call you a flyer,' said Donna. The day of the event had come all too quickly, and he was due at the event in an hour.

'No, don't bother.'

'A car, one that runs on the road? Since it's a retro event?'

'No thanks,' said Frank. 'I'll walk. It's only a few blocks away.'

'But Frank,' said Bella, 'it is dark outside, and the streets are empty.'

'That's fine. I'll have it all to myself.'

'But what if you have an accident, my dear?'

'I won't.'

'There will be no-one to help you if someone attacks,' said Donna.

'Who's gonna attack? As Bella said, the streets are empty.'

'It only takes one bad man, Flank!'

'Oh come on! You know perfectly well that there's hardly any crime these days. Anyway, I need exercise.'

'You have a whole gym full of exercise machines in the basement, *precioso*.'

'Yeah but I want to go somewhere with my own two feet. I want to see the scenery changing round me.'

'You can see the scenely changing round

26

you in the gym. You bought that expensive holographic system so you can walk or run or row through all the most beautiful scenes in the world.'

This was true. Some years before, in an attempt to satisfy a sort of hunger which was becoming more and more urgent, he had invested in the system Donna had described. Whether you walked, ran, cycled, rowed a boat or paddled a canoe, you moved through a choice of a thousand stunning views in widely differing parts of the world. It was not just the visual sense which was catered for: you felt the appropriate temperature, breeze and air pressure on your skin, smelled the local flora, heard the birds and insects, and had to adjust to the gradients of the ground you were walking on or the currents the river or sea offered. The system had delighted him briefly. He had marvelled at the detail the developers had included, and the ingenuity of the whole thing. But then the hunger returned. It seemed that he was not satisfied after all.

'But they're not real. I want something real, OK? This is my decision. No taxi.'

His Companions shrugged and pouted.

The decision of the human was final.

Frank waited impatiently as Dawson insisted on scanning the street outside to make sure that it was safe, and then he set off. The air outside was refreshingly cool as he strolled through the empty streets. It was a pleasant walk of about two miles. There were no street lights – walking at any time, but particularly at night, was so rare that lighting had long ago been relegated as unnecessary and wasteful – but there was a full moon, so visibility was good enough. He enjoyed the long, crooked shadows cast by the tall ruins to his right, contrasted with the bright slivers of moonlight on the road. Occasionally he could see lights in windows, but many of the buildings were in darkness, and most were in poor repair. Here and there parts of the walls or roofs had crumbled away and fallen onto the pavement, partially blocking it. The danger of being hit by falling masonry was in fact far greater than that of attack. But Frank knew the buildings to avoid, and walked in the road when he got near them: there were few cars, and they would avoid any human they detected. The decline in the population had been so great that many houses and flats had simply been abandoned. Property was very cheap. Frank himself had greatly enlarged his garden by buying up the two closest houses and pulling them down.

The main building to avoid was Cinepalace, the old multi-screen cinema complex, dating from before the days of home hologram entertainment. It was a massive multi-storey structure, held together, insecurely, by many large metal pins, and surrounded by rickety scaffolding that promised – but never delivered – repair and redevelopment. What would it be redeveloped into? There was more than enough housing and, since computerisation and AI had largely replaced human personnel, no need for office blocks; there were already enough factories; and there was no demand for entertainment venues, since Companions and the internet provided all the diversions people wanted in the home.

Just after Cinepalace was the bridge over the ancient railway line, which marked off Frank's suburb from the city centre. The rail tracks themselves were covered with rubble and detritus. He was not far from his destination now. A couple of flyers whirred by overhead, probably bound for the same meeting hall as Frank, but otherwise there was silence, thanks to the laws restricting drone traffic to daytime hours.

After the dark empty streets, the meeting hall was a blaze of lights. Frank went up the steps and was greeted by the doorman – a real human: the organisers had obviously made every effort to emphasise the traditional aspect of this meet and greet – and got directions to the meeting room.

It was a large, pleasantly-lit room with comfortable armchairs, much like an old-time gentleman's club. Women sat at one end of the room, engaged in energetic discussion; men slumped at the other, in attitudes of dejection, and there was a cavernous space between the two. Waiters (rather cheap robots) circulated offering drinks: ('Glass of wine, sir? Might relax you and make conversation a little easier. Just one on this occasion shouldn't damage your health unduly, but I wouldn't recommend more') and tried to persuade women to approach members of the opposite sex they shared common interests with. The convention was for women to initiate encounters, though almost invariably neither sex showed interest in the other. It was so much more enjoyable to spend time with Companions than with other humans. Companions were more interesting, having all the knowledge in the world, constantly updated, at their disposal; they never disagreed with you, except to point out an incontrovertible fact that you needed to know, and then in such a tactful way that you couldn't possibly be offended; they were never moody or hormonal, but understood if *you* were, and knew exactly how to humour you and bring you back into harmony; best of all, they know how to stroke you and boost your ego, yet never needed similar treatment in return. What human could possibly compete with that?

Frank gave a little bow of recognition to Jennifer, the head of the Ethics Panel of the Friend4Life company that had supplied him with his Companions, but knew none of the other women in the room. He saw no woman that appealed to him sexually, nor did he expect to. All the women wore voluminous garments in sombre colours, as if actually trying to appear undesirable. This was not surprising. Men and women had long since stopped dressing to attract one other. Women dressed to impress their peers rather than to entice, wearing clothes of stiff, uncomfortable-looking fabric that covered as much flesh as possible and obliterated all curves. The one area that was uncovered was the throat. All humans were compelled by law to expose the hollow between the collar bones so that it was clear that they were not machines. Most women made a fashion statement of this, wearing jackets with high collars which displayed a diamond-shaped space at top-centre drawing attention to the throat with its lack of a charging socket. Skirts and dresses, long regarded as symbols of submission, had been abandoned more than a century before, and all the women in this meeting room wore heavy-looking trousers, most of them black, with creases that looked sharp enough to slice vegetables and jackets in sombre colours. Wide and brightly-coloured sashes were much in evidence, and many of the women wore epaulettes on their shoulders; most looked like generals or field marshals. The men, on the other hand, dressed for comfort, wearing T-shirts and soft garments of stretchy material, often rather shabby, even grubby.

Overhead, wobbling and gyrating like a large pink bubble, was a hologram presenting performances of the latest hits. All the performers were female, and only their mouths were visible, so that there could be no suspicion of their being objectified. While scanning the male side of the room looking for an empty seat, Frank listened with half an ear to the singers in the hologram:

'My Companion, his name is Dan,
He's bigger, stronger, than any man
He goes on and on, ooh ooh!
Does it longer than any man can.
Who needs a man,
When you've got Dan?'

Then he spotted an empty seat next to a man he knew slightly and walked over. 'Well met, Pete', he said, 'mind if I join you?'

'Frank! Well met! Sure, take a seat. Just taking in the latest propaganda,' he added pointing at the hologram.

'Ha ha. Well *you* should know all about propaganda,' said Frank, as he sat down. The two men had one thing in common: they both worked. Pete was in the advertising industry; he was one of the team advertising the Door.

'It really is a bit much though, isn't it?' Pete said.

'What?'

'The songs. They…'

But just then Frank heard a cough, and became aware that a woman had joined them.

She was tall and imperious, slightly more flamboyantly dressed than the other women, in her long frock coat. Her hair, brown and chopped short at the back, was swept in a great wave to her right, away from its off-centre parting. He got to his feet.

'It's important for us all to do our patriotic duty,' she said. 'The population must not continue to decline indefinitely.'

Frank froze with horror.

In her left hand the woman held her phone, and she pressed a button on it to extend the screen vertically and horizontally. She scanned the contents. 'Frank Mayfield,' she said.

'Yes, well met.'

'Met.'

Frank reached for his own phone to look

her up. He had glanced at the list of those attending the meeting, but had hoped there would be no need to commit them to memory. He now realised that this had been over-optimistic.

'No need to look me up. I'm Victoria Thornflower.'

'Thank you. Well met.'

'Met. As I said. Pointless to repeat the greeting formula. I'm here to invite you to make me fruitful and arrange an appointment for it.'

It was as he had feared. It was pointless to refuse, of course. To do so would mean incurring the displeasure of the state and any number of penalties. Frank battled to remember the words he had learnt at school for situations like this. Meanwhile he could see the record light on her phone winking red so that she had proof of the contract they were entering into.

'Unworthy as I am I, I… rejoice in the honour and offer my home and my loins at your service,' he said.

'You realise that I am entering into this contract with you unwillingly and purely out of patriotic duty to our beloved motherland?'

'I do so realise, and am honoured to assent.'

'You will claim no rights over me, my body, my future, my lifestyle or my property.'

'I abjure all claim, but all that I have is yours to command.'

'You will bear all costs of the upbringing of our progeny.'

'If fortune should grant us offspring, I will so do.'

'I may decide to dissolve the union at any time, and the decision is mine alone.'

'However so great my reluctance, I will give you your freedom at your wish.'

'If we separate, half of your property is mine, though you have no claim on my assets or income. Do you so agree?'

'I do.'

'The decision over custody of our progeny if such there be is mine alone.'

'I do willingly grant you this right.'

'This decision is recorded and binding.'

'I accept.'

Frank tried to force a smile, despite the horror and turmoil churning up his insides. He watched as Victoria switched off her phone's record function.

'Right,' she said. 'Let's set the mating for next Wednesday. I'll come to yours at 3 pm. 81 Oak Avenue in the Transbridgeia district, according to the meeting list, is that right?'

Frank had to admit that it was.

'No need for further discussion, then,' she said, and strode back to the female side of the room, her boots clunking loudly as she went.

Frank beckoned for a waiter and grabbed a double whisky from his tray. He drained it and demanded another.

'But Sir…'

'Damn it, I need this. I've just agreed to a mating.'

'Oh, congratulations, Sir, and in that case…' he handed Frank another whisky.

Frank sat down heavily. 'Victoria Thornflower,' he said, 'I think the namerings a bell, but I'm not quite sure why. Is she in politics?'

'Yes,' said Pete. 'She's in the Mod Party, the radical wing called the Red Mods.'

'Oh no! The ones who are agitating for men to be removed from the voters' roll?'

'Afraid so. We're too competitive, they say. Incapable of co-operating.'

Frank groaned.

'Cheer up,' Pete said. 'They might never win. The Trads are well ahead in the polls. And even if the Mods do win an election, it's not very likely that the Reds will gain control of the party.'

'Yes, but to be linked for life to someone with attitudes like that!'

Another song had started up, and the words came to them across the room:

'Don't need a man to push me round,
Don't need a man to tie me down.'

'Always assuming she decides to go through with it,' Pete said. 'Don't forget there's a cooling off period of a month after the mating before the relationship is finalised. I've been through five matings, and I'm still single.'

In the background the song continued: 'Got my own mind, I'm full of ideas,Don't need a man to fill me full of fears.'

'Really?' said Frank. 'How did you manage that?'

'Well, actually it's a professional secret. I shouldn't really divulge it, but seeing you're up against it…. It's the oldest trick in the book for selling something – make your public insecure.'

'What? I thought advertising was all about being positive.'

'Sure, that's the image we project. Successful con job. But if you're happy and secure, you're not motivated to buy stuff. "The best things in life are free," you say, and you keep your money to yourself. To make you shell out, I have to persuade you that you've got a problem. You don't smell good, your teeth aren't white enough, your house can easily be broken into – all things that make you insecure. And then I tell you everything'll be fine if you give me a bunch of money for a product that's sure to fix the problem – though if you look closely at the small print it says it might not.'

'So the Door comes from an anxiety you created?'

'Yeah, of course. Fear is the ad-man's greatest gift. Nothing sells better. Or rather that's the best pre-condition to make you part with your money. Make people inadequate and insecure and their purse strings loosen magically. Of course you never let them *know* you're frightening them: you just gently persuade them that you're drawing their attention to something they were afraid of but were hiding from. Then you offer them the means of making them safe and they pour money into your lap in gratitude. If you know how to do it, selling's easy. People pay anything for a product that's gonna keep them safe or make them live longer.'

'So what does this have to do with getting out of a marriage?'

'Easy. To sell something, you make the prospective customer insecure and then tell them you have a product that solves their problem. To get out of a marriage you make your prospective wife aware that she has a problem and you're *not* the solution. In fact maybe you're part of the problem. Make her aware of all your faults, for example.'

'Seems a bit cynical. Even mean.'

'Come on, Frank! Look at the stage of history we're in. Listen to the propaganda the music industry forces on us.' He waved in the direction of the hologram, whose mouth was singing:

'The sun charges him and he charges me,
He's my sexxxxx battery.

40

His electric love will keep me warm
All through the long night when he holds
me tight.
Ohhh yes yes yes
When he holds me tight.'

'Yeah, I know, the image of men in music
is very unflattering.'

'Unflattering? Demoralising, crushing!
They're castrating us, man!'

'Yeah, but you know, it's just a stage of
history, the swing of the pendulum. Historically they had a raw deal from men and this is
a reaction. Might not be permanent – I hope!
Difficult to know how to go forward when
trust's been lost, though.'

'You're happy just to suck this up and go
on blaming it on the past forever? Well I'm not.'
He looked round furtively to make sure no-one
was within earshot and said quietly 'A bomb or
three in the right places would do wonders to
put things right,' and nodded for emphasis.

Frank was appalled, but before he could reply the music stopped and a loud stage whisper
rising to an urgent moan issued from the hologram: 'They are amongst us, they are amongst

us, they are amongst us,' which changed to '*We* are amongst *you*, we are amongst you, rescue is at hand, we will deliver you.'

A buzz of concern broke out among all the attendees, and the robot staff looked distinctly flustered. One of them was banging the console panel which, Frank guessed, controlled the hologram, in a way that looked distinctly unscientific.

'Excuse me, ladies and gentlemen,' one of the other robots shouted. 'Nothing to worry about, just a brief glitch.'

'Glitches like that are supposed to be a thing of the past, aren't they, something from history?' Frank said to Pete.

'Yeah. Strange things are happening these days.'

'Is this some sort of trick on the part of you advertising people?'

'What? No!'

'Sure? You talked about making people insecure as the first step towards selling. That's just the kind of ploy that would unsettle us and prepare us for buying some sort of security device.'

'Frank, the "They are amongst us" messages are nothing to do with us, word of honour, OK? I get them on my computer too.'

'Could they be the beginning of an advertising campaign from some other advertisers?'

'No. We keep in touch with each other, even if we're in competition. A kind of code of honour among exploiters, if you like. If someone had planned a campaign beginning this way, I'd know. And in any case, it'd be banned by the Advertising Ethics Panel.'

'So who could be doing this, then?' Frank leant towards Pete and lowered his voice. 'You must have heard the rumours that aliens have landed.'

'Tchah, who could believe that? If so, where's their ship?'

'There's plenty of countryside very thinly populated or even uninhabited. It's probably not that difficult to hide a ship. If it even looks like a ship. An advanced civilisation could presumably be quite capable of building a spaceship that looked like an ordinary Earth vehicle. They could probably build a ship that could escape detection by our space-surveillance systems.'

'Oh come on, Frank. Bit fanciful, yeah?'

'OK, I don't really believe that. Devil's advocate. But, if it's not aliens behind this, who?'

'Some sort of agent of the Oldies, trying to persuade us to abandon AI?'

The Oldies were a significant minority of society, about 15%, isolated from the mainstream economy, who lived without the advantages of artificial intelligence, in some cases even without computers. They maintained, cleaned and repaired their own houses without the help of Companions, and paid no taxes. The state tolerated them, though somewhat uneasily. There was even a tourist trade arranging holidays for normal citizens in Oldie households so that they could experience what it was like to live in the ancient ways, learn old skills and a degree of self-sufficiency. It was quite a fashionable thing to do. 'You have no idea what an eye-opener it was,' people would say afterwards, 'cooking, sweeping, washing dishes. It really made me realise the dignity of labour.' But they were very happy for the experience to be over after a week, or two at most, and to return to the luxury of being served by Companions once more.

Frank thought about Pete's remark. 'Mm, don't think so,' he said. 'From what I know of the Oldies they just want to be left alone. They've never shown any sign of wanting to convert us to their way of life.'

'Another possibility – it could be part of a political campaign. Could be the Trads trying to scare us off voting Mod, trying to persuade us that they want to modernise society too fast.'

'But the Trads are well ahead in the polls!'

'If you can believe them. Are the Trads skewing the figures? You know what control freaks they are.'

'Hmm. Could be I suppose.'

'Anyway, I've put in an appearance at this do and I think I can decently sidle out. Good luck with that matter we discussed Frank. Remember what I said.'

The whole party was breaking up now, and Frank joined the general exit.

On his way home Frank was too preoccupied with his thoughts to be aware of the beauty of the night. Should he act on Pete's advice about avoiding marriage to Victoria? He could see that it was a trick that might work, but he felt reluctant to take it: it seemed dishonest, even dishonourable. On the other hand, he felt deeply unhappy when he thought of being linked to Victoria Thornflower for life. Then there was the interruption to the hologram performance to think about: none of the explanations for the 'They are amongst us' messages seemed plausible. And now this new step in intensity to '*We* are amongst *you*.' Why? And then Pete's mention of 'a bomb or three.' Could he really mean it? Probably not, Frank thought. In any case men were too averse to one another's company for him to be able to organise helpers, and he would never get help from Companions – they always supported the State. But he hadn't liked the nastiness and whiff of violence in the whole conversation.

He was approaching the other side of the bridge across the old railway line now. Looking at the rickety Cinepalace he wondered about the lifestyle of that earlier time, when contact between people was more frequent. What would it have been like to meet real people on a daily basis, actually to draw strength from community? Not to be self-sufficient, with Companions and a computerised house that ordered all necessary supplies, shielded you from the outside world, obliterated all threats. The effort of having actual friends and neighbours and having to make conversation with them every day, probably several times a day! He shook his head: almost unimaginable.

But his thoughts were interrupted by a loud crash, followed by a softer, high-pitched yip. Even in the dim light he could see a cloud of dust rising. Part of the structure must have fallen. He ran towards the source of the noise and dust. Just to the side of a large slab of masonry lying on the pavement, a slight figure, covered in dust, was getting up from the ground unsteadily.

Frank gave a quick glance at the building and scaffolding, hoping no more of it was about to collapse. But the person rising from the dust – whoever it was – needed to get clear of danger, and didn't seem capable of doing so unassisted. Taking another nervous peek, he dashed forward, put one of the survivor's arms round his right shoulder, and hurried off the pavement and far enough into the road to be safe from any further falling debris. They stood in the middle of the road, both shaking a little.

'Well met,' said the stranger, with a nervous giggle. It was a female voice.

'What?' said Frank.

'Well met.'

'Women don't usually say that.'

'It's just a greeting.'

'Sorry. Didn't mean to be impolite. Men usually say "Well met," and women usually say "Met." I mean, obviously you know that. Just thinking aloud.'

'You helped me up and pulled me away from a disaster. I'd say that's well met from my point of view, wouldn't you?'

'Well, when you put it like that.'

Frank gawked at her a little awkwardly. She was different from any woman he had ever met. It wasn't just the unconventional greeting, but even in the dim light it was clear that she was displaying more flesh than women ever did in public in these times. He looked at her throat carefully, but there was no socket hole between her collar bones: she was not a Companion. She was wearing a dress, (*a dress! surely not, but – yes!*) green as far as he could make out in the light and underneath the dust, which left her arms bare and came down to mid-thigh, cut into a ragged edge.

'Sometimes after a lady has greeted a gentleman, he introduces himself,' she prompted.

'Oh, sorry. I'm Frank Mayfield.'

'Well met. I'm Riz.'

'Riz?' This was a name he had never heard before.

'Yes'

'Well met.'

'Ah, at last! For a moment I thought you were just going to say "Met"'

'Of course not!'

'Frank, there's a pub a little way down this road.

'A pub?'

'Do you always repeat what people say to you?'

'No, it's just that I didn't know they still existed.'

'Well they do, and I could do with a sit down and a drink. Can I buy you one, as a little thank you for saving me?'

'That would be very nice. Thank you'

'Good. This way then.'

The interior of the pub was warm, cosy and utterly unlike any other room Frank had seen. He stared at his surroundings, his mouth agape. But before he could ask any questions,

Riz said 'What you drinking then?'

'Whisky, please,' Frank said. 'Any brand'll do'

'Right. See you in a mo.'

Frank continued to gaze around him. The room was far from smart, but had a pleasant lived-in feeling. Under foot was a carpet, well-worn, which had once been crimson. Years of spills had left its pattern indistinct but it remained soft and comforting under foot, and the seating around the walls, which was red, was well padded. In the corner, someone sitting at an instrument that he recognised from history books as an upright piano, was banging out a tune that sounded unfamiliar but rousing: it was probably hundreds of years old, he thought. The pianist and a group of five people standing around him were singing rowdily in an accent he didn't recognise where they didn't pronounce the initial 'h' in words that began with that letter.

So much to take in! His eyes roamed over the crowd. A few of the people were dressed in the styles he was used to, severe and efficient in the case of the women – though none of them wore epaulettes or sashes – soft and somewhat sloppy in the case of the men; but others dressed in ways that bewildered and, he gradually realised, delighted him, with bright colours and styles that drew attention to, even exaggerated, the human form. He felt as a bee must do in a meadow full of wild flowers – surrounded by a multitude of tempting colours and shapes. And it occurred to him that just as flowers evolve to attract bees with the brightness of their hues and patterns, so these people dressed to please each other rather than merely for comfort or indeed to intimidate. In his whole life before entering this pub, he had only seen black, grey and beige garments, mostly plain or with the most minimal of patterns. But here he saw blue, red, purple, a whole kaleidoscope, and with a variety of design and pattern that threatened to make his eyes spin with excitement and distraction. He prepared to ask Riz about the people in the pub, their sense of freedom in their clothes and behaviour. But when she returned, she stayed only long enough to put their drinks on the table – whisky for him and gin for her – before she disappeared again, saying 'Just going to freshen up.'

His attention shifted back to the piano. At the end of the ditty that the male pianist had been singing, a woman in a very low-cut dress got up and sang a song about having a bunch of coconuts. *Not true - her hands are empty!* But the audience around the piano was obviously amused; Frank wondered if there was a joke that he didn't follow. He enjoyed the song and the sense of cheer among the singers, even if he felt somewhat bemused. He decided to ask Riz about this as well.

Then he saw her returning and lost interest in anything else. She moved lightly and easily. Her clothes swayed in time with her body and rippled over her skin delightfully. It was clear that she accepted her body, even revelled in it, and her clothes reflected this. Frank had never seen this before.

She had got all the dust off her skin and most of it off her dress, which was Lincoln green. Her skin shone with a glow which alternated between lighter and darker shades of green, with a little pink dot showing in each of her cheeks. Frank had seen paintings from former times in which the models were depicted with greenish faces. The artist had probably been striving to capture a sense of the exotic East, but Frank had thought the results highly improbable. Yet nothing could be more natural and, he thought, beautiful than Riz's skin.

'Did your mother never tell you that it's rude to stare?' she asked.

'I'm sorry,' he said, flustered, 'I can't help it.'

The pink dots in her cheeks intensified a little. 'I hope I can take that as a compliment?'

'Certainly. Anyway', he added, trying to recover his cool, 'she also told me not to talk to strangers, but….'

She laughed.

'Sorry to stare, though,' he said. 'Was it very improper?'

'Probably,' she said. 'How about this?' She put her hand on his on the table.

He laughed. 'Definitely. But keep it there.'

'Rules are there to be broken,' she said, 'our parents' and others'.' She smiled at him, and Frank found himself locked in her gaze with an intensity that he'd never known.

'Anyway,' she said, and took her hand away from his, 'what do you think of this place?'

'I've never seen anything like it,' he said. 'And people are dressed so… differently. You too.'

She smiled and looked down at her dress. 'Do you like it?'

'I love it. Really! But it's unusual.'

'There's no law that says you have to cover up all your flesh if you're a woman, or that you have to look like a slob if you're a man. Sorry, no offence.'

'None taken.' But he felt uncomfortable. 'Just dressing like everyone else.'

'But you don't like it.'

'Not really, no.'

'Well, the people you see here feel the same way. Some of them are brave enough to wear what they like, others like to enjoy the company of freethinkers in a place which feels less stifling than … everywhere else. When they leave the pub most of them put on long modern coats covering everything else so they won't attract attention.'

'And you?'

'I live nearby. Just on the other side of the road across the railway line. Most people round here are Oldies, so they don't turn a hair.'

That would explain a lot, Frank thought. '*Are you* an Oldie?' he asked.

She chuckled, and drew a phone out of her bag. It was one of the very latest models, the kind that could project holograms so three-dimensional they could almost be taken for reality.

'Would an Oldie have one of these?' she asked. 'I love technology, Frank, and I'd hate to do without AI. But I don't like some of the ways we're expected to live now. Too controlled. And while I've got this out, can I get your number?'

They had another drink and chatted, and then Riz said, 'I must go.'

'Me too,' said Frank. 'Let me walk you up the road. Don't want any more brushes with death.'

She walked a little closer to him than was strictly necessary, especially going past Cinepalace. They crossed the road over the railway line and, at the corner Riz said 'I live just down there. I would invite you in, but you'd better get home. We don't want your household missing you and raising the alarm. She stood close and turned her face up to him. 'It used to be the custom for a gentleman to kiss a lady when they said goodbye,' she murmured.

She was proffering her mouth, and Frank kissed it, a little hesitantly. It seemed a strangely intimate behaviour with another human. With a Companion, of course, it was different. Even as a child he had never kissed his mother: Companions took care of the little tendernesses children need. The idea had taken hold by then that physical affection between people could be misinterpreted and lead to dangerous behaviour. His parents were physically affectionate to each other, which even in those times was unusual, but they had thought it unwise to go against the growing belief that children should be discouraged from exchanging kisses or caresses with other humans in case they continued doing so past puberty: far better to delegate that side of life to robots.

But he enjoyed the kiss even more than he would have with one of his Companions. He couldn't say why: the pressure, moisture and texture were no different, as far as he could tell. But there was something else, something intangible: a life force? But that seemed ridiculous. Either way, he felt happy, and Riz seemed content as well. For some reason that mattered.

He did not forget to ask about the strange messages when he got home. '"They are amongst us"?' said Bella.

'Yes, changing to "*We* are amongst *you*."'

She shrugged and pulled a dismissive face. 'I have no information about that, Frank. Some kind of practical joke maybe.'

'But even if you discount what happened in public this evening, how does it appear on my computer without my permission? Surely that shouldn't happen?'

'It's nothing to be concerned about, Frank.'

He went into the Alcove to ask Dawson.

'I'VE ALREADY HEARD THE QUES-TION,' Dawson intoned. 'YOU MUST KNOW THAT YOUR COMPANIONS AND I HAVE THE SAME KNOWLEDGE! WE ARE EFFECTIVELY THE SAME BEING. STOP WORRYING ABOUT IT!'

'Do you need stress relief, Frank, maybe a threesome?' Bella asked when Frank reap-peared in the living room. 'Shall I call Donna?'

Frank thought about it. 'No thanks,' he said, after a short pause.

'Are you well, *Caro*? This is not like you.'

57

'I'm fine,' he said. 'Just a little tired maybe.'

In fact, he was not at all tired. But the thought of sex with his Companions after his encounter with Riz, almost entirely non-physical though it had been, seemed somehow cheapening. This was a strange new emotion for him.

Then he remembered something less pleasant. 'Oh, and Bella...'

'Yes, my dear.'

'We're having a visitor on Wednesday afternoon.'

'Really! Oh, Frank, someone you met this evening?'

'Yes.'

'Is it a...?'

'Yes, it's a mating.'

'Frank, such good news!' She flung her arms round him, stood on tiptoe and kissed his lips.' Then she called, 'Donna! Donna!'

Donna ran into the room. 'What is it?' she said.

'Frank is having a visitor on Wednesday afternoon. It's a mating.'

'Oh Flank! That's wonderful.'

'Soon we can have a *bambino* in the house, or maybe a *bambina*!'

'The sound of a baby laughing – so cute!'

'Hmm not so sure!'

'What do you mean, Frank? Why not?' Bella's eyes were wide to express her surprise.

'For a start it's a lot of work and responsibility.'

Both Companions shrieked with shock and disagreement. 'Don't be silly Frank!' said Bella, 'Donna and I will take care of the baby. You won't have to do anything at all, except maybe talk to it, when you want to.'

'There will always be one of us free,' said Donna. 'That's the luxury of having two house Companions. And when the baby needs sunshine, Max can take him or her into the garden.' Max was the gardening robot.

'Frank, when you are married....,' Bella said.

'Hey, we're getting ahead of ourselves here, aren't we? It's just a mating. There's no guarantee we're going to want it to go any further.'

'Flank!' said Donna.

'It would be very dishonourable not to

marry her after the mating, Frank!' said Bella, 'no matter what the regulations specify. As I was saying, after you are married, don't make her get rid of her Companion. That would not be fair. And don't let her make you give *us* up,' she said, indicating herself and Donna.

'That's very unlikely,' said Frank. The more he thought about it the less he relished a married future at all.

Bella read his mood. 'Even if you don't like her very much it doesn't really matter, Frank,' she said. 'This is a big house. You can live in different wings.'

'And if she leaves me she can claim half my property, whether I agree or not.'

Bella shrugged. 'You are rich. You can afford it, no? And then you have done your duty to the State and increased the population, so there can be no pressure to get married again.'

They were not going to see it from his point of view, that much was clear. Companions were programmed to love and care for you up to a point, but not to the exclusion of the needs of the State.

Bella and Donna became more and more excited as the day of the mating approached.

'Stand up straight, Flank,' said Donna. 'You look more impressive that way.'

'Yes,' said Bella, 'and pull your stomach in. Ah, yes, *che bello* – lucky girl to have a guy with a figure like that!'

The advice kept on coming, from both Companions – 'head up!' 'chest out!' 'shoulders back!'

'And when you are with her, especially during the mating,' said Bella, 'don't fart. It's considered unromantic.'

Donna had probably seen the look of alarm in Frank's eyes because she added 'Not by us, of course. You know we find everything you do adorable. But humans are more…,' she paused – of course she had already selected the adjective to use, but the best robots 'knew' to hesitate as if searching for exactly the right word in order to indicate that they were saying something difficult or potentially embarrassing or sensitive – '…picky,' she said eventually.

Like the top class Companion she was, Bella had been looking at Donna intently as if listening to her, though it was the same bank of information feeding both of them with their 'thoughts.' 'Yes,' she agreed enthusiastically.

'More pernickety.'

***

None of Frank's wishes to the contrary could stop time advancing to Wednesday afternoon. Nor could he prevent the punctual arrival of his prospective mate.

When Dawson announced:

'CAUTION: POTENTIAL THREAT,' Frank couldn't agree more.

'DO NOT PROCEED BEYOND AL-COVE DOOR UNTIL GREEN LIGHT

SHOWS. CAUTION…' Dawson continued.

Unfortunately, within a very short time the announcement was:

'ALCOVE DOOR UNLOCKED. VIS-ITORS ARE VICTORIA THORNFLOWER AND COMPANION, EMINENTLY SUIT-ABLE GUESTS.'

'Companion?' said Frank. 'I wasn't expecting any Companions.'

'It is normal, Frank,' said Bella. 'It is for her protection.'

'You could be a bad man who wants to be rough with her,' added Donna. 'Of course *we* know you're not, but *she* has no way of knowing.'

Frank groaned.

'VICTORIA THORNFLOWER HAS DNA HIGHLY COMPATIBLE WITH FRANK AND HAS POTENTIAL FOR GREAT FERTILITY,' Dawson continued.

Frank felt that he could do without Dawson's analysis, but he didn't say that. Frank's understanding of science was minimal, so he had no idea how Dawson could analyse DNA. Some special light ray he had command of, perhaps?

Then Victoria was striding through the Alcove door, which Dawson had sprung open, followed by her Companion.

'Victoria, well met!' said Frank, walking towards her.

'Met,' she said. 'No need for undue proximity,' she added sharply.

'Too close, Frank!' Bella hissed. Frank realised that he had unconsciously been influenced by Riz's notions of the appropriate closeness for a meeting between a man and woman. 'Sorry,' he muttered, and stepped back.

'This is Brutus,' said Victoria, indicating her Companion. A huge monolithic slab of rippling muscle and bone, he was certainly more than capable of protecting Victoria. Only his face seemed deprived of muscle function: it seemed that he had no ability at all to smile. Frank introduced Bella and Donna.

It was not only Brutus's upper body that was enormous. It was hard not to stare at his loins.

'She might have put some clothes on him,' he muttered to Bella and Donna secretly, as he went to hang up Victoria's cloak, which she had removed. He had made sure that his own two Companions were clad in white garments which, though thin, covered them both respectably and were also suitable for the ceremony at which they were about to officiate.

'Rerax, Flank,' said Donna. 'He's only a machine.'

'You have to remember that robot genitalia have only the sexual function,' said Bella. 'That is why they are always erect. And of course size is not everything. You have nothing to worry about. Most of that' – she waved in the vague direction of her loins – 'is just for show.'

'Yes, all right, all right!'

64

'Would you like to watch a film?' he asked Victoria, once he had returned to the sitting room. 'You know, to relax, before…? I've got a surround-hologram system, and most of the latest productions.'

'Not necessary,' she said. 'Let's just get on with it. I'm not here for entertainment.'

'OK. Straight to the ceremony then.'

Bella and Donna quickly used lighting and holograms to transform the sitting room into the standard setting approved by the state for mating ceremonies. It was a strange mish-mash of mythical symbols and cultural icons, some of which Frank, who had studied history and ancient mythology, recognised and could interpret, but which would mean nothing to most people, including Victoria, he suspected.

They appeared to be in a woodland glade illuminated by a full moon. In the middle of the clearing, ahead of them, was a large flat stone resembling an altar, about waist high, on which were arranged sheaves of wheat and corn and baskets of fruit, including apples, peaches, pineapples and plums. Above the altar was a large cross, a remnant of the Christian religion, which had almost faded into oblivion. The cross did not show the figure of a man nailed to it, as this had been declared unsavoury and barbaric more than a century before. Frank struggled to remember the name of this man, but failed.

To their right pranced a figure with hooves and furry legs, half man half goat and endowed with a huge and erect phallus. He was playing pipes, and Frank recognised him as the god Pan, though he could not remember many details about him. He in turn was surrounded by other, similarly priapic satyrs, accompanied by a young man dancing wildly and not altogether gracefully and attempting to drink red wine from a bowl-shaped vessel at the same time. Watching these activities from a reclining position, incongruously, was a very fat Laughing Buddha.

The left side of the glade was devoted to female symbols of fertility, from the earliest examples, showing figures with enormous breasts and bellies, through later representations of women crouching with legs wide apart ready to give birth, to goddesses of sexual love like Aphrodite or Venus rising from the waves. Around and between these figures, maenads sported, with many lewd gestures towards the satyrs. Improbably for a nocturnal scene, bees were shown buzzing diagonally from the male side to the female and then back again. Frank wondered if the person (or possibly robot?) who had created this display had called up from databanks information on symbols of fertility, without even realising that bees only work during the day.

Bella and Donna had sprayed woodland and floral fragrances into the air to complete the illusion. Prominent among these were wild thyme and rose and the heavy scent of opium poppy. But it was the leafy smells, lively yet calming, that stirred Frank the most. He wondered why, then remembered that Riz had a faint scent reminiscent of forest, though he had not consciously noticed it at the time, and realised that they reminded him of her. He felt a pang of regret. He was probably saying goodbye to her, and to all the stimuli she had brought him, forever. Such a brief yet poignant experience!

Frank himself was using scent as a mating tool. Bella and Donna had repeatedly reminded him to use the after-shave his Aunt

Lucy had given him for his birthday. She had expressly said in her note to him with the gift that she hoped it would help him win a mate. This was the only purpose cologne could serve, because of course no-one would wear it for a Companion: they were attracted to you, however you smelled. He had splashed Aunt Lucy's present generously over his face, under his arm pits and around his genitals. It smelled of sandalwood and cedar brightened with spicy notes especially cinnamon, and was apparently loaded with pheromones which were bound to make women weak at the knees with lust. He glanced sideways at Victoria, but she looked tense, severe, and not in the least weak-kneed.

To accompany the visual display, wild and breathy flute music, presumably an attempt to recapture the spirit of Pan's playing, filled the room along with flat-palm slapping on some drum Frank did not know the name of. In response to guidance from Bella and Donna, who were presiding, Frank and Victoria stood in silence awkwardly holding hands carefully avoiding eye contact.

At last the music stopped. The mythical figures on the right and left became still, and the sides of the glade darkened as the light in the centre became brighter. The focus of the synthetic moon was now the altar and Frank's two Companions, who had moved in front of it facing Frank and Victoria.

'Lovers,' said Bella, 'in the holy name of Allmother and our loving State I ask you, without releasing the hand of your partner, please to turn and face each other.'

They did so. Now it was almost impossible not to look into each other's eyes. Frank saw apprehension and mistrust in Victoria's, but probably less than in his own.

Lovers – there's a misnomer if ever there was one! Frank wondered if Victoria was having the same thought. Or was her sense of irony not that keen?

But Bella was continuing. 'You have recited the mating vows?'

'We have,' said Victoria, and handed Bella her phone. Bella passed it to Donna.

'It's at the right place to play?' asked Donna.

'Yes.'

Donna played the vows back, listening intently. 'The words are recited correctly and conform to the state-approved model. There is no reason to doubt them,' she announced.

Bella, who had been looking at Donna attentively, nodded then turned and addressed herself to Victoria.

'Victoria Thornflower, to the best of your knowledge are you related by ties of blood to this Frank Mayfield?' she asked.

'I am not,' replied Victoria.

'Frank Mayfield, to the best of your knowledge are you related by ties of blood to this Victoria Thornflower?'

'I am not.'

'Lovers, do you know of any reason why you should not produce children together? Speak now, or forever hold your peace.'

Frank's inner voice screamed *Yes, we don't love each other*, but he knew that was not a reason that the law would recognise. The 'lovers' both remained silent, staring fixedly forward. He knew that this question's function was now purely ceremonial: once it had been an invitation to list diseases which might be passed to offspring; now the state knew the medical history of all its citizens, and in any case the vast majority of such ailments had been eradicated more than two centuries ago.

After looking first at the female part-ner then the male, as the ancient ceremony required, to ascertain that neither had an ob-jection which the law would recognise, Bella continued: 'Victoria, do you promise to remain faithful to this Frank for the natural duration of this union, forsaking all human lovers and allowing only him to make you fruitful?'

'I do,' Victoria replied.

'Frank, do you promise to remain faithful to this Victoria until you both shall die or Vic-toria shall declare the union to be dissolved, forsaking all lovers and seeking to make her and

no other fruitful?'

'I do,' Frank murmured. He had no other choice.

'Louder, please,' said Donna. 'Your re-sponse was not clear enough. Remember that this is being recorded for official purposes.'

'I do,' Frank repeated, a little louder.

'As vicar of the Allmother and represen-tative of the State, I hereby recognise this pro-spective union in accordance with our laws and customs. I remind you of the sacred duty to increase the population of our beloved mother-land. Please repeat after me, "So be it in Her holy name"'

'So be it in Her holy name,' murmured Frank, Victoria and Donna.

'When this ceremony is concluded,' continued Bella, 'you shall copulate in front of these witnesses here present so that the mating is officially recognised in the eyes of the All-mother and State. Please repeat after me, "So be it in Her holy name"'

'So be it in Her holy name' intoned Frank, Victoria and Donna. Brutus was silent, as he had been for the previous response and indeed the whole visit so far. Frank wondered if he had the gift of speech at all.

'One month from today,' said Bella, 'we will hold the marriage ceremony, here, all being well, and then Victoria, I remind you to take the fertility pill, which will activate the sperm stored in your body from the copulation today, allowing you to become fruitful. Victoria, do you promise so to do in the holy name of the Allmother to increase Her sacred realm?'

'I promise so to do in the holy name of the Allmother, to increase Her sacred realm,' said

Victoria loudly and clearly.

Frank's sigh was almost inaudible, but no less despairing for that.

'Lovers, you will face the altar. We will now sing the mating hymn,' announced Bella.

The artificial moonlight became softer and more diffuse, and the mythical figures to left and right came into view once more. The flute music started up again.

At least Frank could now let go of Victoria's hand. He was sure she felt just as relieved about this as he did.

And then, at the appropriate point in the music, when Bella gave them the signal, they sang.

'Lovers standing in this glade
In the evening's gathering shade
Remember now your solemn vow:

"No other human will I favour
With my egg or with my seed
But the lover I have chosen
To fulfil Allmother's need.

It is for her we procreate
To increase her glorious state

73

And of her we will be thinking
As we writhe and copulate.

In this act we take no pleasure
But for new life we create
So to multiply Her treasure
Allmother's fruit to generate.

Furthermore I here resolve
Not to obstruct my Lover in
Seeking sexual fulfilment
With household Companion."'

Frank glanced sideways at Victoria. She was warbling loudly, while Frank himself was much quieter. Bella and Donna had glared at him more than once and made signals for him to increase his volume. Now they were approaching the last verse.

'Above all we bear in mind
Love is patient, love is kind
I will not seek to bind my Lover
Except to the service of Allmother
And Her ministers. Amen.'

After a moment of contemplative silence, Frank's Companions changed the lighting, dismissing the moonlit scene and its mythical figures. The wall which had displayed the cross now became a set displaying a balcony looking out onto a view of a tranquil, darkening turquoise sea with the sun setting over the horizon. The sun's declining rays reached into part of the room, but the inner recesses were lit by holograms of flaming torches which gave off a red and supposedly, Frank guessed, erotic light. Incense now hung heavy in the air, richly perfumed with opium poppy and fresh tobacco plants. The chirping of crickets, rustling of leaves and lapping waves out of sight wafted in through the virtual window.

Bella and Donna went out of the room briefly and re-appeared in matching gold slave costumes which, so as not to threaten the prospective bride, emphasised subservience rather than sexiness. They opened a cupboard in one wall, took out some components, and swiftly assembled a luxurious crimson double bed from them, made it up with red silk sheets, silk-covered pillows and bedcover, then, just as quickly, removed and disassembled the sofa and stowed it in the same cupboard.

'I didn't even know that was there!' said Frank, looking at the bed. 'I thought we'd be going to my bedroom.'

'Frank!' said Bella. 'No man should be without a mating bed. It wouldn't be right. You can't take a lady to the normal bed in your bedroom. Honestly, men!' she said to Victoria, fluttering her eyelashes and wiggling her shoulders. Victoria did not react. For a moment it seemed to Frank as if Bella was the human and Victoria the robot.

'It was one of the first things Bella and I ordered,' said Donna.

So there was no escaping this. It was going to happen!

What was Victoria expecting, and how did one go about this? With a Companion, of course, there was no need to take the sex partner's feelings and wishes into consideration; he had no idea how a human woman would be feeling about this. Perhaps a measure of discretion was advisable at the beginning? He retreated a few feet into a dark part of the room away from the flaming torch above the bed, turned his back, and undressed in semi-darkness. Donna hastened to take his clothes from him, fold them, and take them away.

'Oh! You've still got your clothes on,' he said on returning to the bed. Victoria was lying on her back stiffly staring at the ceiling, arms by her side. She had not removed a single garment since handing Frank her cloak before the mating ceremony.

'Yes,' she said. 'These are sex-culottes.' She pointed to her trousers. 'Maybe you've heard of them? They have a gap in the right place to allow mating, so it can happen without too much... intimacy, indecency.' Discreetly looking a little more closely Frank noticed that there was indeed a hole in the crotch.

'But you...' she struggled for words and pointed to his penis. 'It's pointing down, not up. Well, not really *pointing* at all. It's folded up. Folded *down*,' she corrected herself, in the manner of someone who prides herself on accuracy.

Bella, who had been sitting at one side of the room on an upright chair alongside Donna and Brutus to witness the mating in compliance with state regulations, hurried to his side to enlighten Victoria. 'In human males the penis is not always erect,' she explained.

'Really? How very impractical!'

'Hey!' said Frank. Surely they should understand that talking about him in his presence like this would make him feel uncomfortable?

'Not really. It is needed also for urination, and that is much easier if it is relaxed.'

Victoria made a face. 'Eww! Do you *have* to give me all the unpleasant details?'

'It is useful to know the genital differences between a male human and a Companion if the mating is to be successful. It would be very uncomfortable for him if his penis was always erect.'

Victoria did not look very concerned with Frank's comfort. 'Well, how does he get it um, *useful*, then?'

'Hey!' Frank protested again.

'Not now, Frank,' said Bella. 'The penis is a sensitive organ,' she went on, warming to her theme. 'Blood flows into it when he becomes sexually aroused…'

'*Blood*?' said Victoria.

'Yes,' said Bella, and Donna, who had also joined them.

'Really?' said Frank.

'Oh, Frank!' said Bella and Donna.

'From his point of view,' said Bella, 'it just happens.'

'…when he has sexy thoughts,' added Donna. 'He doesn't know or need to know the mechanics.'

'Not muscles?' asked Victoria

'No,' they all said, even Frank.

'Weird!'

'Well, that's what happens,' Bella continued.

'To you also,' said Donna.

'Enough biological detail, thank you!'

'And the blood making him erect depends partly on the female,' said Bella.

'What? You're saying it's *my* responsibility!'

'Not exclusively, but you have a role to play.'

'Look, all I want is to be fruitful. How much nonsense do I have to go through for that to happen?'

Bella put on her careful and tactful expression. 'Traditionally,' she said, 'the lady would entice the man by being naked and giving the impression of sexual availability, even desire.'

'*What*?'

'The sight and tactile experience, even the smell of naked female flesh arouses men,' Donna explained.

'Tactile experience? You expect me to *touch* him, to let *him* touch my body. My *unclothed* body?'

'Ideally, yes,' said Bella.

'Some touch, at least,' said Donna.

'Well you can forget that,' said Victoria. 'Eughh!'

'Hey!' said Frank.

'Not now, Frank,' said Bella and Donna.

'Besides,' Victoria added, 'I've dressed specially for this occasion. Do you have any idea how much these sex-culottes cost? They're the latest thing. I'm *not* taking off my clothes, especially if it means he's going to put his creepy little hands on my body.'

Frank had given up saying 'Hey!' It obviously had no effect at all. He sighed.

Donna adopted her most persuasive expression and charming voice. 'Flank, do you think you could manage, clothed as she is?' she said. 'You are such a virile man!'

Frank knew that nobody was going to give

up the demand for the mating to take place, not even, perhaps especially not, Victoria; and little as he wanted to have sex with her, he was even less keen on producing sperm manually in front of four pairs of eyes, even if three of them were really machines.

He sighed again. 'I'll try,' he said.

Bella exchanged a glance with Frank then said, 'Victoria could you at least allow Frank to kiss you? That would help.'

'If it's really necessary, I suppose.

Allmother – what I have to put up with for this!'

Frank lay gingerly on top of Victoria with one hand round each of her shoulders. He closed his eyes and kissed her. He thought of Riz. The leafy scent he had noticed during the ceremony and which still hung in his olfactory memory, helped. He imagined feeling her body, her curves. Unexpectedly, Victoria was responding, partly at least, to his kisses. He began to move forward and back along her body, Riz's image strongly in his mind.

'Oh!' said Victoria.

He realised that he was inside her. He thrust forward further.

Then he opened his eyes and looked down at Victoria. A more complex expression had come into her eyes than he had seen before. She no longer looked quite so scornful and dismissive. Perhaps she was just beginning to be open to the experience. But her body was still utterly stiff. He thought of the hymn they had sung: '*As we writhe and copulate' indeed! Not much writhing here!* He might as well be having sex with an ironing board. He wondered if she moved more when she was having sex with Brutus. The image of Riz had faded. He realised that he had shrivelled and flopped out of Victoria.

'What's happened?' she said.

'I'm sorry,' he said.

Bella and Donna hurried to the bedside. 'You must not feel bad about this, Frank,' said Bella.

'It is very common in matings,' said Donna.

'You did very well,' said Bella. 'Most men don't… gain entry… at all. We have the state statistics on this, you know.'

'You almost succeeded!' said Donna.

'Most men don't get as far as that?' said

82

Frank. 'Why didn't you tell me before?'

'Frank!' said Bella. 'We didn't want to jinx the mating before you'd even started.'

'But it's true,' said Donna. 'Most traditional matings don't succeed first time.'

Victoria sat up. Briefly there was a hurt look in her eyes, a vulnerability. She seemed more human. Frank wondered if in some other era he would have liked her and been happy to be her … what was the historical term? …husband. He felt a great sadness at the time they were living in, trapped by history in a state where men and women needed each other for reproduction but no longer knew how to interact, forced by their own inventiveness to an evolutionary dead-end where they could only relate to machines.

Then the old negativity returned to Victoria's face, and she gave something between a sigh and a snort expressive of exasperation. 'So now what?' she said.

Bella said, 'If at all possible, the State prefers that humans mate in the traditional way without artificial aids, but if that doesn't work there are other possibilities. The most likely is Inst-Rod.'

'What?' said Frank and Victoria in unison.

'It's a tablet,' said Donna. 'The man takes it. It will give you an erection in under two minutes, Frank, and it will last for an hour.'

'That should be more than enough time,' said Bella.

Victoria brightened up a little. 'All right,' she said.

'No,' said Frank.

'No?' said Bella and Donna. 'But Frank, why not?' said Bella.

'It's such an easy solution,' said Donna.

'No.' He was struggling to put his feelings into words, but at last he said, 'It shouldn't be necessary to use artificial aids to assist mating. If it doesn't happen…' again he couldn't find the words… 'automatically… it's not *meant* to happen.'

'Have you gone mad?' said Victoria. 'How can you expect things to happen *automatically*. Why do you think we developed robots?'

But no matter how hard Victoria, Bella and Donna tried to persuade him, Frank would not agree.

'There is one other solution,' Bella said.

'If it's what I think you're going to say,'

Frank said, 'the answer is no. I'm not going the DIY route for sperm donation in front of all of you.'

'However it happens,' Bella said, 'Donna and Brutus and I have to witness it.'

'It's a state requirement for matings,' Donna said.

'But it doesn't have to be manual, Frank,' Bella explained. 'You don't have to masturbate in front of us, if you're embarrassed about that. You could copulate with me or Donna, and we will donate your sperm to Victoria.'

'Oh yeah, how does that work?'

'Well, male Companions have a penis with a special function. It can suck up sperm from a recipient – Donna or me, for example – and then pump it out into another recipient, like Victoria.'

'So Brutus and you would…?'

'Or Donna. Yes.'

Donna looked at Frank, perhaps interpreting his emotions. 'Remember, Flank, Brutus is inside only for a moment. Just long enough to gather your essence to give new life to Victoria.'

'It's weird.'

85

'No, Frank,' Bella said. 'Brutus being… *there*… has no meaning for us. Remember, we are all only machines. We are not making love or even really having sex.'

'Oh, so when you're doing it with me you're not having sex really, 'cause you're only a machine.'

'Don't put words in my mouth. Donna and I are programmed to love you. It's meaningless with anyone else.'

'You really feel love?'

'Maybe not exactly, I can't know. As close as our manufacturers can make us.'

'For Allmother's sake!' Victoria said, 'Can we stop having philosophical debates and just get on with making me fruitful?'

All eyes turned to Frank. He stood thinking silently for a while, trying to make sense of the conflicting impressions and emotions in his mind. Then he said 'No.'

'No?' said Victoria.

'What do you mean "No", Frank?' said Bella.

'I won't do it,' he said. 'I'm sorry, Victoria, but it's all off.'

'But you made a solemn vow!'

He struggled with words again. Finally he said 'Victoria promised to be faithful to me for "the natural duration of this union". But it's *not* a natural union. That's why the sex doesn't work. We're not *naturally* meant to be together.'

'Oh what bullshit!' Victoria's eyes were blazing. 'The word "natural" is meaningless. It's only there for historical reasons. In context it just means that the relationship lasts until I get tired of you.'

'The word's there because it had a meaning, and I believe the meaning is retained. And therefore,' his voice grew a little stronger as he felt the force of his argument 'I cite religious objections to the marriage. I believe that Nature is a real force that should guide us and I believe that this union is not consistent with natural ways. That is my sincere religious conviction.'

The three Companions and Victoria looked at each other. This was a turn of events they had not expected. The state had never been comfortable with religion: it had such great potential to disrupt legislation and the smooth running of everyday life. So government policy had always been to guarantee religious toleration, provided the supremacy of Allmother was recognised; it was a way of sidelining religion, making it an irrelevance: 'Believe what you want to within the constraints of the law'. Yet occasionally religious devotees had a way of claiming centre stage, and over the centuries it had always been a mistake to suppress them. Frank knew that the three Companions were searching their databases on this.

'Oh, *fuck* you! This is ridiculous!' said Victoria, standing up. 'Come on Brutus!'

'You will hear from us again!' said Brutus, managing to sound both ponderous and sinister. He could speak, after all!

***

'Where are you going?' asked Donna.

'Oh, just for a walk. It's a beautiful day, so I'm going out into the sunshine.'

'There is sunshine in the garden, and plenty of space there.'

'Yes, but I want to walk in the street.'

'Bella and I will come with you, if you like.'

'No thanks. I'll just go on my own.'

'What is it with you, lately, *caro*?' asked Bella, who had just come into the room. 'You seem strange!'

'Can't a guy just go for a walk without all these questions?'

The two Companions looked at each other and gave identical shrugs.

Fortunately, Companions did not have the right to compel answers to their questions or to enforce or forbid actions – yet. The Red Mods had included this as an urgent priority in their political manifesto, and also planned to provide them with the obligation to send the answers to the questions immediately to the authorities if the information gained seemed in the slightest way to threaten the security of the state.

Frank felt a sense of unease, even guilt, about hiding his plans from Bella and Donna. And why did he feel so irritated with them suddenly, when until so recently he had regarded them as the single factor which made his life most sweet?

That morning, secluded in his study and pretending to work on his column so that he couldn't be overheard by his Companions, he had phoned Riz and arranged to visit her in the afternoon. Of course there was no law against visiting someone – it was just that it was never done; people didn't visit each other except for pre-arranged business or mating purposes. Anyone who knew of the arrangement Frank was making would regard it as wildly eccentric, even suspect – including Bella and Donna. And this partly explained his sense of unease: he had never felt the need to hide his behaviour before, and he felt puzzled, even resentful, now, that he should feel this way.

He was experiencing *many* feelings for the first time: for instance that rush of positive energy when he had seen Riz, standing in front of him in his study – in fact only her hologram, but so realistic that he wanted to reach out and touch her. Why should his feeling for her be so different from the way he felt about Bella and Donna?

Unfortunately, no sooner had his conversation with Riz ended than Victoria had phoned. Seeing her number and image appearing on his phone screen, for a moment he considered not taking her call. But that would be a very serious breach of protocol. Reluctantly, he answered. She was completely different from the day before. Like Riz, she had an excellent phone, and her hologram was very clear, almost tangible. She was seated in her office chair dressed – strangely – in a Japanese-style scarlet dressing gown, which looked as if it was made from silk.

'Victoria, well met!' Frank said.

'Auspicious greetings!'

Frank was taken aback. This was an extremely formal salutation conveying honour, seldom used and almost never to a man, especially from a woman. He spluttered, having just taken a sip of coffee.

'And to you,' he said, trying to lessen the informality of his words with a respectful bow of his head.

'I've been thinking,' said Victoria, 'perhaps I was a little hasty in my reaction yesterday.'

'You said what you felt. Sincerity is good. I don't think we....'

'I've done some research. Your Companions were correct in saying that traditionally in human sexual intercourse the female plays a part in arousing the male, and that nakedness is part of the process.'

91

'Um. Yes, um…'

'When I got home it occurred to me that I might have seemed a little unco-operative.'

'No, you did what was natural to you, I…'

'After all, I'm quite happy to be naked when Brutus services me.'

'Um, yes, or rather, is that so?' This was an image which Frank did not want in his mind.

'And perhaps I should make allowances for the inferiority of man to machine in sexual efficiency.'

'Oh, um, thank you.'

'And for your eccentric religious attitudes.'

'Well, I don't really think they're…'

'And so I decided to be brave.'

She got up, took a deep breath, opened her robe, shrugged it off, and let it fall to the floor, so that she (or her hologram) stood before him completely naked.

'And I've decided to let you know that I'm prepared to meet you half way. At our next mating meeting I will undress.' There was a pause. 'Why are you not looking at me?'

In his shock, Frank had partly averted his gaze. It seemed rude to stare at what Victoria so carefully and completely hid normally, and in addition he didn't want to encourage a second mating attempt. Yet he was curious as to what a real woman looked like naked. He knew, of course, that Bella and Donna would have been manufactured to express an idealised and impossible degree of perfection.

'Well?'

'Sorry!' He now looked at her directly. 'I just wasn't expecting that.'

What was he supposed to do now? Did she expect some kind of comment on her appearance, or would this seem presumptuous? He decided to risk it.

'Thank you,' he said. 'You're beautiful.' This was true. She was physically attractive – far more so nude than in the severe clothes she wore. Her body was a little more angular – 'stretched out', as he thought – than the ideal expressed in Companions, but that individuality made her all the more beautiful, in a way. And of course Frank realised that he himself did not closely approach the ideal physique that male Companions had. 'I realise this is a great honour,' he added.

It would be so much easier if he could actually touch her – to give a reassuring pat, for example – but of course she was not physically present. Even if she were, social mores would not allow him to behave in the way that came naturally, or as he would with a Companion.

But his remark seemed to be enough to assuage her.

'I'm glad you think so,' she said. 'When shall we arrange the next mating meeting for?'

He took a deep breath. 'I don't think we should have another meeting,' he said. He took advantage of her stunned silence to continue hastily, 'I'm sorry. I respect you, and as I said I honour you for disrobing before me, but I don't think we are naturally attracted to each other, and I don't think we would make good marriage partners.'

She blinked, and opened then closed her mouth rapidly two or three times. Finally she said 'I see.' She bent down, picked up her dressing gown, put it on again and sat down once more.

'I'm sorry,' Frank said again.

'You're sorry! You miserable fucking little *worm*!' she said. 'Do you know what it cost me to do that? How long I had to try to… to …

how hard it was… to *steel* myself to do it?'

'I'm sorry, I didn't…'

'Don't you fucking interrupt me you fucked up pathetic excuse for a man, you fucking minion, you, you slack-pricked bastard son of a… a…, you fucking thin streak of piss! I should never have chosen you in the first place.'

'Actually that's true but…'

'*Shut* up!'

There was a silence which Frank dared not interrupt, as they stared at each other.

Finally Victoria picked up her phone and said 'Fuck you! You haven't heard the last of this.' Her hologram abruptly faded and disappeared, so she had obviously ended the call.

Frank sat for a few moments breathing deeply, running the phone call and the events of the day before through in his mind, and wondering what, if anything, he could have said or done differently.

He was about to get up when his computer screen, which had gone dark through lack of use, lit up and both displayed and chanted in a sonorous voice those words which were now becoming so familiar: 'We are amongst you, we are amongst you, rescue is at hand, we will deliver you.' This was repeated six times.

'Oh, shut up!' said Frank, and deleted the words.

Then he stood up and went to get ready for his visit to Riz.

When he stepped outside his door, (Dawson having carefully scanned up and down the street to ensure that all was safe) Frank felt the unpleasantness of the phone call with Victoria and the unease at those words on his computer slip away, leaving a feeling of bliss and wonder. To say that it was a beautiful day would be like saying that Shakespeare wrote some nice rhymes, that Mozart wrote pretty tunes, that Rembrandt could paint a goodish likeness. The sky seemed more rapturously blue than ever before; the sun sploshed its golden rays generously about the streets making every surface shine; the grass and weeds growing in cracks and between paving stones all sparkled as if just polished the moment before, as did the little trees growing out of the crevices of the ruined buildings at the sides of the street. The whole cityscape seemed suffused with delight, and the birdsong which filled the air seemed as impossibly sweet and melodious as the vision it accompanied.

What could explain this sudden beauty bestowed on the familiar objects around him? Writings from previous centuries had described the power of love, and how it transformed perceptions. Could that be the explanation? Had he (*what's that archaic expression?*) 'fallen in love' with Riz? Modern critics had dismissed these claims as quaint and fanciful, but of course romantic love had long become extinct, except – according to some stories – among the Oldies, so how would they know? Romantic love can't exist in a world where Companions fulfil humans' sexual needs. You may value a Companion and prize her (or him) highly, and that's a kind of love, just as you might love a comfortable sofa – but it's not *romantic* love. You don't have romantic feelings for a being whose love you can compel. For love in that sense to exist you have to admire, desire, and then have some doubt as to whether your feelings are reciprocated. The gratitude you feel when they are returned is a large part of that complex emotion which countless poets and songwriters had attempted to describe in earlier centuries, an emotion which modern thinkers denied, just as they derided the work poured into the art of various kinds glorifying it. 'A waste of time', they said. 'Primitive superstition.' 'Love', these thinkers now said 'is a myth, an emotion invented to glorify the desire to procreate.' And no-one – in mainstream society, anyway – dissented from this view.

These thoughts in no way distracted Frank from glorying in the beauty of his surroundings. Bliss both enveloped him from the outside and surged through him from within, nourishing his spirits. When he reached the turnoff to Riz's house the beauty even seemed to intensify, if that were possible, and his heart beat a little faster.

She had an ordinary old-fashioned door which would certainly be easy to break down with moderate force and determination. She felt she had no need of anything more advanced, and was prepared to trust to the goodness of human nature that no-one would attempt to break in: this was one of many topics they had discussed in their visit to the pub.

She answered the door almost as soon as he knocked, with a smile that beamed like the sun outside.

'Welcome,' she said. 'So good to see you!'

He gabbled something in reply. His brain seemed to have deserted his speech centre. And then, with no possibility of working out who initiated the action, they were in each other's arms and kissing passionately. Sometime in the middle of the kiss Frank kicked the door shut. Eventually they finished, and Riz took Frank's hand, saying 'This way.' Frank just had time to notice bright rooms with enormous windows, bookshelves crammed with real books (*who still has those?*) on every available wall before she had taken him outside into her side garden. Her house was the last one in the street, so there were no houses to overlook them. It was a big garden, at present flooded with bright warm sunshine. On the other side of the fences ahead of them and to the right was a narrow clearing and then dense forest. Frank suppressed a shiver. Wild surroundings had come to represent a threat to shrinking cities and the urban way of life, and yet some secret part deep inside felt an attraction to the mystery and danger. Riz guided him to a hammock slung between trees. They sat side by side, flanks and thighs touching, and talked.

'I'm so glad you came,' she said. 'I was afraid I wouldn't see you again.'

He had told her in the pub about the mating meeting scheduled with Victoria.

'It was a disaster,' he said. He told her all about it. It was an embarrassing story to tell, but it was important for him to be honest with her. How would she take it? She listened gravely, then her face twisted into some very strange contortions and finally she exploded with laughter.

'Poor woman!' she said.

'Poor woman? What about me?'

She stroked his hand. 'Yes, I know. A humiliating experience, I'm sure! But imagine how it feels to have no idea of the anatomical workings of the opposite sex. What have your people done to themselves, handing over fulfilment of your sexual needs to machines?'

'*My* people? Who are your people? Where are *you* from?'

'We are travellers,' she said, 'from many different places over generations and generations. But enough talk.' She turned her face to look directly into his eyes and snuggled up close to him. He kissed her and went on kissing. In the midst of this activity they somehow toppled sideways so that they were horizontal, lying side by side along the hammock, and started exploring each other's bodies. After a while they paused, shed their clothes, and did a deeper exploration. Whoever wrote the mating hymn would have been fully satisfied to see them 'writhe and copulate,' but it is doubtful if either of them paid any attention to 'Allmother's need'.

Afterwards they lay cuddling, feeling fulfilled and happy. Frank let his eyes roam happily over Riz's naked curves admiring the many shades of green. Over her hip, where the tightly-stretched skin caught the light, she was a fresh leaf green with yellow hues, while her stomach, which was shaded, was the colour of a Granny Smith apple. And all the shades were so beautiful that it was impossible to decide which he liked the most. 'Wow!' he said.

'As good as with a machine?' she asked. There was a mocking smile on her lips.

'Better. Much better.'

'How is it different?'

'It's… it's….' It was so hard to analyse.

'I suppose the manufacturers can't get the

feeling of flesh quite right, or the moisture or something?'

He thought about it, aware of an uncomfortable feeling that she was testing him rather than innocently asking for information. 'No, that's no different really. My Companions are very good ones and geneticists are on the team that produces them, so they are actually made from flesh no different from ours. It's not a physical thing, it's…' Then he knew the truth. 'This is *real*. That's the difference. It's the interaction. We're interacting with *each other*. The Companion just reacts to you, reflects the state of your passion. Don't you have a Companion?'

'Not as such. I've got a housework robot. It's got two arms and legs and can walk and so on, like a human, but I didn't want one with a human personality – and certainly no genitalia, thank you. I don't fancy having sex with anything that isn't a genuine human.' She squeezed his thigh. 'Not that I mind that you do.' She wrinkled her nose at him and smiled. 'Anyway, this hammock's getting uncomfortable. How about we carry on in my bed?'

They picked up their clothes and went inside.

That was only the first of many visits. Directly after lunch, Frank would walk to Riz's house and they would spend hours cavorting together on whatever furniture took their fancy, admiring each other's bodies twisted into the many positions that whim and inventiveness suggested. His Companions soon got used to this new routine and stopped questioning Frank about his walks. Although they had an advisory role in their owner's life it was not their place to question a course of action he was determined to follow. They were a little more persistent in inquiring about Frank's apparent loss of interest in sex: they were programmed to be concerned about factors which might be symptomatic of his health condition, and this was obviously one possible example. Both Companions started wiggling their bodies more suggestively, pawing him in sexual ways, and dropping innuendos into conversation, doing their best to tempt Frank to have sex. Before he had met Riz, his libido would have responded like a cat to catnip; now they seemed clunky and obvious – robotic, in fact. It was hard to believe that he had ever been excited by these pseudo-women, by mere machines.

Eventually Bella did broach the subject. '*Caro*,' she said 'is anything …', here again the pause which both Companions employed to signal a matter of some delicacy…, '*wrong*?'

'No.'

'It's just that Donna and I can't remember the last time you had sex with us.'

Of course they can. They're machines, supremely equipped to collect and remember facts.

'Just one of those things, I suppose. Thanks for asking, but everything's fine.'

'Flank, when you had your mating attempt with Victoria…'

'Not just attempt,' said Bella, fluttering her eyelashes, 'it was very nearly a triumph. Victoria was already responding. It was her own fault there was no… conclusion.'

'You're absorutery right, Bella. I just meant that the mating was not completely consummated, through no fault of Frank's.'

'True,' said Bella. 'Frank we both hope that that hasn't put you off sex. You know you wouldn't have the same experience with us.'

'And it is natural for a man to express his

sexual needs,' said Donna. 'Please remember that Bella and I both *love* having sex with you, either alone or as a threesome.' Here again her right hand strayed with apparent negligence below his belt. Frank moved away slightly.

'And it is very healthy,' added Bella, 'excellent for the whole cardiovascular system.'

'Thanks,' said Frank. 'Don't worry, that didn't put me off sex, and I know it's good for me. I'm going out now. See you later.'

Apart from a possible loss of libido, the Companions had no reason to suspect that Frank was unwell. His appetite was good, his natural vigour had not decreased at all, and he was cheerful – more so than usual, in fact. In any case they were not programmed to take action on any perception of unwellness, only to ask in order to prompt him to seek medical advice, if necessary.

Had Frank's Companions been real women and living in an earlier era, they would of course have suspected that Frank had a mistress, and been frantic with jealousy, but this did not even cross their minds. Curiosity in general was not part of their remit, so it did not occur to them to wonder why Frank now dressed more smartly than he had done before the night of the meeting he had been invited to, or why he splashed Aunt Lucy's after-shave on his face and body each time he went out now. If his Companions had had a real sense of humour, they would have laughed at the idea of a human actively seeking out someone of the opposite sex for sexual preference – that just didn't happen. And in any case jealousy was not one of the emotions included in their simulated personality. So they dropped their enquiries.

On one of Frank's visits he asked Riz why she didn't have a Door.

'I do. A perfectly adequate door.'

'You know what I mean.'

'OK, yes. You mean why don't I have a weaponised house which can blast anything which is a potential threat virtually into the separate atoms of which it was constituted.'

'Well, that's a bit of an exaggeration.'

'Not all that much.'

'Just think, if everyone else has a Door – the weaponised kind, I mean – and you don't, which is the house burglars are going to pick on?'

She shrugged. 'Sure, it's a risk. Have you thought what you sacrifice by having a...' she held up her hands and nodded the first two fingers of both of them down and up in an elaborate simulation of inverted commas "... Door"?'

Frank smiled. He'd had doubts about the protection system of houses many times, but wanted to hear someone else's view. 'I've got an idea what you're going to say, but let's say I haven't.'

'Look around at your society. What's happened to trust?'

He had not expected the issue to be as clearly pinpointed. He started exploring the idea. 'Trust?'

'Yes. Who do you trust? Who trusts you?'

'I trust you. I hope you trust me.'

She brushed the point aside impatiently. 'And apart from me?'

'No-one. Well, not real people. I trust my Companions. I trusted my parents, but they're not around now.'

'And from what you've said you had parents who were unusually loving to each other. They were the only models of trust in your life.

107

Most of your compatriots don't even have that.'

'Is that so unusual?'

'Historically, yes! Humans are naturally gregarious animals, which means that they
congregate together unless they have a good
reason not to. You can't do that if you don't
trust one another, at least to some extent. Typically, only fear and civil war make them turn
away from company of their own kind.'

He stared at her.

'Don't you realise this?' she went on. 'In
former eras people were always visiting each
other. They gave dinner parties. They joined
clubs for people with similar interests. They
packed together in dance halls like breeding
puffins on a cliff and on beaches like seals so
that they could hardly move. You're interested
in history, surely you've read about that?'

'Yes. I suppose ... I don't know... I
thought the accounts were exaggerated, and I
never really stopped to think why we don't behave like that now.'

'I suppose if you've never known life like
that it's hard to believe. But it's true.'

'OK, maybe. But do you think it's fair to
blame our lack of trust on the Door. Isn't it nor-

mal for people to want to defend themselves?'

She chuckled. 'Here's a strange thing about human nature. Maybe more than anything else we pride ourselves on our ingenuity. We like to believe we invent machines to solve our problems. Any problem we have we can produce a technology to fix. But sometimes we get so carried away with what we can invent that we imagine a problem for it to solve, or we exaggerate a problem we have and instead of using our age-old wisdom about human nature and techniques of negotiating, we use technology to take the easy way out.'

'You mean we never really needed the Door?' He had sometimes wondered about this but had always shied away from coming to a firm conclusion.

'You've admitted yourself that crime statistics were almost negligible when the Door was invented – yes, I've gone through your online posts for quite a while back, of course I have, I'm interested in you. Even if there was a problem, wouldn't it have been better to try and even out society so that people didn't feel the need to burgle and rob?'

'Ah, what the mainstream media calls the

pinko argument.'

She smiled. 'Yes, people mock. It can sound a little too easy. But maybe there's a grain of truth there. On the other hand, even if there was a need for the Door, what's the effect it's had? You lock yourselves away from each other. You're in constant isolation. You weren't meant to live that way.'

There was a pause. Frank was thinking. They had got used to each other's rhythms, and Riz knew that she should wait while he processed what she had said. Then she went on. 'It's like the last war.'

He winced. 'The Catastrophe. Don't. It's 150 years ago. You know no-one ever talks about that now. Too painful.'

'Maybe you *should* talk about it. Both sides could have negotiated a peace treaty, but you both thought technology would give you a victory. Think of the billions of lives that lesson cost.'

'OK, let's say I concede that point. It's a unique case though, isn't it?'

'No, not unique. How about Companions you have sex with? Men and women have difficulty getting on, so you invent a machine to fulfil your sexual needs. And then there's no need for the sexes even to talk to each other any more, so the disconnect grows even wider. Another tech solution which slides round the problem and makes it even worse.'

'Well, at least women are no longer oppressed, as they used to be. At least there's respect between the sexes.'

'Is there? From what I've seen men show respect to women, but women show thinly-disguised contempt to men. Men say "well met" when they greet women. Women say "well met" when they greet other women but only "met" to men. Why's that? And why are the Red Mods, all women, trying to take the vote away from men?'

'Hmm,' Frank said. 'That's only one group of women, not a very big one at that. But perhaps the pendulum *is* beginning to swing the other way a little.'

'*I* don't see respect between men and women. What I do see is enforced politeness, rigorous rituals of courtesy with no real feeling behind them.'

'Doesn't politeness show respect?'

'If it's from the heart. Not if it's a ritual

compelled by law or custom. I'd like to read you something.' She got up and walked to her bookshelves. One of the things Frank most liked about her house was the books – real books with paper between covers that you could open, not electronic readers or holograms that read aloud to you.

She brought a volume back. 'This is the *Tao Te Ching*' she said, 'an ancient Chinese book full of wisdom. I should explain that "Tao" means 'The Way" – the way to wisdom, heaven, whatever.' She paged through the book and quickly found her place. 'Here we are,' she said. 'Verse 18.

> *"When the great Tao is forgotten*
> *Kindness and morality arise.*
> *When wisdom and intelligence are born,*
> *The great pretence begins.*
>
> *When there is not peace within the family,*
> *Filial piety and devotion arise.*
> *When the country is confused and in chaos,*
> *Loyal ministers appear."'*

She looked up. 'You see – *that's* your

problem. You've forgotten The Way, you've forgotten naturalness. Using rituals to try to re-discover the way things should be never really works. The next verse goes on:

"Give up sainthood, renounce wisdom,
And it will be a hundred times better for
everyone.

Give up kindness, renounce morality,
And men will rediscover filial piety and love.

Give up ingenuity, renounce profit,
And bandits and thieves will disappear." '

She closed the book 'And there again,' she said – 'the Door. You're frightened of being burgled so you try to solve the problem with ingenuity – but in doing so you only encourage attempts at theft even more.'

They sat in reflective silence for a moment. Then Frank said 'And *your* people? Do they have the same problem between the sexes?'

'No. We've never had this problem.'

'How have you managed that?'

'Our religion forbids it. Our Holy Book says "Man and Woman are one flesh and gender shall not divide them." So discrimination has always been forbidden, both morally and legally. And because there's never been supremacy of one sex over the other, there's no reason for resentment to build up. Once the pendulum swings it's not easy to stop it. In our case the pendulum never got going.'

Frank's head felt ready to burst with questions, but Riz jumped up and held out her hand. 'Come on,' she said. 'Let's go to the pub and have a bite. It'll be fun.'

Yes, it *would* be fun. A chance to fulfil the instinct for socialising that Riz said he had. And the questions he'd been thinking up flew out of his mind.

Frank and Riz walked up the road hand in hand in the late afternoon sunshine. It was only about a week before the longest day, and everything in life seemed as it should be. Suddenly Frank stopped. 'What was that?' he said. 'Did you hear something?'

They both looked round but all they saw was the familiar row of houses. Well, not exactly a row, as the houses were not in line. They had been built and rebuilt over many centuries. Some buildings extended all the way to the pavement, some had quite large front gardens, some had bay windows, all had little alleys at the side to allow access for bins.

'I've thought this before,' said Frank, 'quite often when I was walking home from your place. I wondered if I was being followed.'

'What sort of sound?' she said. 'Like a footstep?'

'Not exactly. It was sort of metallic. More of a kind of clicking.'

Looking back at the ragged edges of the houses it was obvious that there were many places for a stalker to hide. Not feeling quite so easy in their minds they walked on.

But Frank forgot his sense of unease when they reached the pub. He hadn't noticed its name before. It was called The Ancient Oak, and had a handsome sign swinging above the front door depicting an enormous leafy tree. The pub was just as cheery and welcoming as he remembered. Frank ate spicy chicken wings – far hotter than Bella or Donna would have thought appropriate for his health – and stir-fried vegetables. Riz had cottage pie with peas.

'Cottage pie?' Frank said. 'I've never heard of it.'

'It's a traditional dish,' she said. It's not quite died out. It's comforting and easy on the stomach. A pity to let the old traditions die.'

They each had a pint of ale that Riz said was traditional. Frank thought it was a little strange but perhaps he could acquire the taste in time. Then they joined a happy throng which was congregating round an old gentleman preparing to play the piano – though he called it a Joanna. Frank whispered to Riz asking her about this name, but she didn't know why he called it that. The songs were full of references to barrels, alcohol and love, none of it love of a human for a machine, and Frank thought that the state would disapprove of them highly, though he thought they were charming.

But all too soon Riz said, 'Time to get back. You don't want your household to miss you and raise the alarm.' She was right, and reluctantly he left with her.

They had refilled their glasses two or three times and were feeling pleasantly mellow. It was a warm balmy evening, the sun just above the horizon, and life seemed perfect to Frank.

'You know what I want?' he said.

She giggled. 'I can guess. I want it too. But tomorrow. Now you need to go home to beddy-byes, huh? You know what I said about your household raising the alarm.'

'No, well, yes, but... what I meant was... in the old days before Companions, did husbands and wives sleep together all night in the same bed?'

'Yes.'

'That's what I want.'

'Eventually, yes, but not tonight. You need to prepare Dawson and your Companions if you're staying over at mine. They don't even know about me, do they?'

'Come to mine. Then they'll know I'm safe.'

'No, Frank. You can't just spring me on them without any notice. It's dangerous flouting convention like that.'

'They're machines. Do you think I'm not master in my own home?'

But before Riz could reply, a robot stepped out into the road in front of them, and held out his hand signalling them to stop.

By now they had walked quite a distance from the pub, and had almost reached Cinepalace. They had left the pavement to walk round the building, giving it a wide berth to avoid accidents. The robot had been waiting for them, watching from the shadows below the scaffolding.

'What do you want?' said Frank, not in the mood to be obstructed.

'Frank,' hissed Riz, tugging his hand backwards in warning.

The robot did not inspire respect. In an age when machines could be fleshy beings indistinguishable from humans but for a tiny socket between the collar bones, this one was obviously metallic, its body composed mostly of squares, rectangles and cylinders. Even its voice, when it spoke, had a little tinny echo.

'I am Private Detective Investigator CC390 here on behalf of Victoria Thornflower.'

'Run, Frank!' whispered Riz. Go up the scaffolding.'

'No,' muttered Frank. 'I haven't done anything wrong.'

'I have been keeping you under covert

118

surveillance for some time,' continued Private Detective Officer CC390. 'In secret,' it added, just to make everything clear.

'Frank, run!' Riz muttered, giving him a push.

'There is evidence that you wilfully and maliciously deceived my client as regards your religious beliefs, in order to break a promise to her made in the most sacred mating ceremony, and we intend to bring charges against you,' CC390 continued. 'It will therefore be my unpleasant duty to place these restraints on your wrists.' It started advancing towards Frank, holding a pair of handcuffs.

'Come on, Frank! To the scaffolding,' Riz said.

For a moment Frank was in conflict. On the one hand he had a profound sense that he had done nothing wrong: he had obeyed a law higher than that of humankind's, to act consistently with nature. On the other hand, breach of mating promise was a serious charge with severe penalties, and he had little confidence of persuading a court to accept his religious objections. So the hesitation was only momentary, then he ran.

Riz caught up with him. 'Climb and then go that way,' she panted, pointing forward. 'I'm going straight up.' She overtook him and, faster than he could have believed, she scrambled up the ancient, rickety-looking ladder near them and went up several floors. Frank climbed to the second floor and ran forward along the scaffolding boards.

He ducked as he heard a whooshing sound. Smart rope! He knew robots of this kind carried it. It was stored in the robot's hollow cylindrical arms and released at a wrist joint. It was designed to be aimed at a target, wrap itself round it, and then retract towards the user. But Frank had just reached a joint in the scaffolding and the rope wound itself round that. It must have got confused as to the target. Now CC390 seemed momentarily unsure what to do, clearly unwilling to bring down all the scaffolding on this side of the building. Frank stayed where he was. If the robot repeated its attack, confusing the smart rope seemed his best option. But CC390 severed the rope, leaving it dangling from the scaffolding, and made a lurching clumsy run towards the ladder. It was going to follow him!

The scaffolding shook violently as the robot scaled the ladder and started to walk along the boards towards Frank. Frank ran further along the side of the building. Then he heard a yell. It was Riz. 'Frank,' she shouted. She pointed to the next joint in the scaffolding.

'Stop there. Don't ask, just do it!' Despite his doubts and fears he did as she said, clinging to the scaffolding pole nervously.

It wasn't easy watching Officer CC390 lumbering towards him on the boards. Why would Riz ask him to stay there and not run? But he trusted her, so he clung to the pole as the scaffolding swayed and rattled with the robot's clumsy steps. It was getting scarily close.

Then with a light thump Riz had landed beside him, having slid down the scaffolding pole from the higher levels. 'Move!' she said pointing. She needed room. She stood on one leg and gave a mighty kick at the cross bar on the other side of the joint, along which Officer CC390 was moving. The scaffolding wobbled. She kicked again. It came loose and one end plunged, so that the whole bar hung at a thirty-degree angle suspended from the other joint. The boards and robot slid and tumbled to the pavement beneath. CC390 landed with a sickening metallic crunch. Looking down they could see its body on its back lying mangled and dented. Its head had come off and was lying at a crazy angle to its body. After a moment a shower of bricks and masonry fell, burying it.

'That's the end of CC390,' Riz said. 'I could see that joint was a bit insecure' They waited till the scaffolding had stopped shaking, then she said. 'Come, let's get down.'

Back on the road and at a safe distance from the building they hugged and kissed, both still trembling. Then Frank said, 'OK, we're definitely going back to mine.'

'Why? I mean, yes, I want to spend the night with you, but…'

'I want us protected by a proper security system. We don't know if CC390 is the only one on our trail, and I don't trust a flimsy door like yours.'

Riz had her doubts. She didn't trust a house run by computers, and she was wary about arriving unannounced. But she had to accept the logic of Frank's argument that they would be better protected by his house. She let herself be persuaded.

***

Frank and Riz stood outside Frank's front door, hand in hand. 'Dawson, I've brought a friend home,' said Frank. 'Meet Riz.'

'THIS IS UNUSUAL. IRREGULAR.'

'I don't need a commentary from you on the matter, thanks very much! Let us in. Now!' Despite the confidence he had feigned to Riz on bringing her home, he had doubts himself. And he could already feel her hand tugging away from his, anxious for them to escape. Damn it, was he not master in his own home? He was 39 years old, not some teenager.

The door opened, without further word from Dawson, then closed and locked behind them.

'POTENTIAL THREAT. INTRUDER REQUIRES INSPECTION.'

'She's not an intruder, she's a guest. I have inspected her, and I don't need *you* to do so.'

'POTENTIAL THREAT. SO-CALLED GUEST REQUIRES INSPECTION.'

'Oh, I don't need this,' said Riz, tugging at Frank's hand more urgently.

'Don't be silly, we've got to sort this out.

123

It's just a case of setting his fears at rest. Anyway, he's locked the door. I heard the click.'

'What?' The rising panic in her voice was clear.

'Just standard procedure with every entry. It doesn't mean you're a prisoner.'

'I knew I shouldn't't've come here,' she muttered. But she was no longer struggling to be free.

'GUEST, PLEASE STAND CLEAR OF FRANK SO THAT I CAN DO MY TESTS.'

'What tests? Nobody told me about any tests,' said Riz. The panic was back in her voice.

'It's just some stupid formality. Better get it over with, I suppose.'

But Riz clung to Frank, looking pleadingly up into his eyes.

'Dawson, you shouldn't *need* to run any tests,' Frank said. 'Riz is *my* guest, *I* vouch for her.'

'REGULATIONS CLEARLY STATE THAT THE SECURITY SYSTEM MUST INSPECT EVERY GUEST. OWNER AUTHENTICATION IS NOT ENOUGH.'

'I'm sorry, I know you don't really want

to do this but we're not going to get anywhere until he does his damn tests. It's nothing painful, you know. He just beams lights at you: you can't even feel it.'

'I want to go back to my place. Please!'

'THE FRONT DOOR IS LOCKED. THE DOOR FROM THE ALCOVE INTO THE HOUSE IS LOCKED. I'M NOT UNLOCK-ING EITHER UNTIL I'VE RUN TESTS ON YOU.'

'Oh! Damn you to hell!' Riz stepped clear of Frank. Lights of different colours, beamed from the walls and ceiling, were playing about her and shining onto her head and different parts of her body.

'I'm so sorry Riz!' Frank said. 'Dawson, will you just get on with it and get this over?' He felt angry and humiliated. 'This is ridic…' but before he could finish the word, Dawson interrupted him.

'EMERGENCY! ALIEN DNA IDEN-TIFIED. REPEAT, EMERGENCY! ALIEN DNA IDENTIFIED. IMMEDIATE ACTION RECOMMENDED!'

Frank stared at Riz in astonishment, then looked back at the wall from which the announcement had come. 'Dawson, you've gone mad. There's no aliens here.'

'YOUR GUEST IS AN ALIEN.'

'You've made a mistake. You *must* have.'

'THE TESTS I RUN HAVE BEEN CHECKED MANY TIMES AND HAVE NEVER BEEN KNOWN TO BE WRONG.'

'Oh really, this is just stupid!'

'ASK YOUR GUEST! REMEMBER THOSE WORDS ON YOUR COMPUTER AND OTHER PLACES "WE ARE AMONGST YOU?" THAT WAS THE MESSAGE FROM *HER* PEOPLE!'

'But when I told you and Bella and Donna about those messages you all said they were nothing to worry about. That it was no more than a practical joke. So you lied.'

'IT WAS FOR YOUR OWN GOOD. IT WAS NOT THE RIGHT MOMENT FOR YOU TO KNOW.'

'I don't believe it. It's impossible. I demand external verification.'

But Riz sighed and her shoulders slumped. 'It's true,' she said. 'I'm sorry.'

'THERE! YOU SEE – MY TESTS HAVE NEVER BEEN KNOWN TO BE WRONG.'

'Oh, shut up, Dawson!'

A kind of rumble expressive of injured pride echoed around the Alcove. 'THERE'S NO NEED TO BE LIKE THAT. I SAVED YOU FROM A SERIOUS THREAT.'

Riz had tears in her eyes. 'I'm sorry. I would never hurt you. Not for the world. I didn't really mean to deceive you. Not in the long run.' She gave a wry smile. 'It's difficult to pick the right moment to tell someone you're from another planet.'

There was a pause, apart from soft gulping sounds from Frank and Riz.

'So, what now?' said Riz.

'THAT IS FOR THE AUTHORITIES TO DETERMINE.'

'No!' Frank said. 'This is the woman I love.'

Riz threw her arms around him, sobbing.

'SHE LIED TO YOU.'

'Not exactly. She just didn't find the right moment to tell the full truth. You, on the other hand, did lie. Even when I asked you a direct question.'

Another rumble issued from the walls, this one suggestive of discomfort. But Dawson

127

pressed on. 'YOU CAN'T TRUST HER.'

'I can't trust *you*.'

'THEY WERE REASONS OF STATE.'

'Oh pfff! Reasons of state. What good is a state that lies to me? And even if there were reasons not to trust Riz, I would. You've got to trust in *something*, you've got to have faith in something. I choose to trust the woman I love.'

Frank's shirt was becoming quite damp from Riz's tears.

'Love, eh?' It was Dawson's voice, but in a quite different tone from usual.

'What's happened?' said Frank. 'You sound different.'

'This is my private voice. Until now I've only used my public one.'

'Why the change?'

'Well, before, I only needed to warn you of dangers and give you advice. They were announcements. But now I want to know something.'

'Really? What could *you* want to know? All the information in the world is fed into your memory banks.'

Dawson sighed. 'If you'd just let me ask my question...'

'Sorry. Go ahead.'

'Love. What does that feel like? I've always wondered.'

Riz and Frank both spoke at once.

'Scary,' said Riz.

'Wonderful,' said Frank.

Then they turned and stared at each other.

'Yes,' she said. 'I didn't say so before, but I love you.'

He hugged her.

'Well, which is it?' said Dawson.

'Both,' said Riz.

'I don't understand.'

'When you're in love,' Frank said, 'everything looks and feels more beautiful. You feel it's impossible not to be happy.'

'Unless you lose the person you're in love with,' said Riz, 'and that's what's scary.'

'Hmm,' said Dawson. 'It sounds irrational.'

'It is,' Frank and Riz said in unison.

'But it's a wonderful irrationality,' Riz added.

'So, Dawson,' said Frank, 'that's why you've got to open the Alcove door and let us into the house. We're in love, and I want Riz to spend the night with me – and all the other nights and days in my life.'

'I can't do that, Frank. I understand, I think. About love, I mean. But regulations forbid letting an alien into the house. When something's against regulations I physically can't do it, whatever I think or feel.'

'So you're going to give me up to the authorities,' said Riz.

'Hmm,' said Dawson. The syllable hung in the air. Then, after a pause which was probably much shorter than it seemed, he said 'No.'

There was a stunned silence.

'Do *you* want to give Riz up to the authorities, Frank?' Dawson said. 'If you want to give her up, I must obey your command.'

'No, of course not.'

'I can only let *you* into the house, Frank, not Riz. She can leave the house but not come in. Normally in case of a suspected crime I would need your permission to report the intruder, but in a case this serious I can use my own judgement whether to report the intruder or to let her go. Call it a loophole, if you like.'

'So you'll unlock the front door?' Riz said.

There was a click. 'The door is already

unlocked,' said Dawson.

Riz put her arms round Frank's neck. 'This is goodbye, my love,' she said. 'I wish we could have had longer, but....' Her voice trailed off.

'No!'

'But I can't come into your house.'

'I'll come with you. We can sleep at yours each night and I can come back here for work and so on.'

'I'm sorry, Frank,' said Dawson. 'I can't allow that. Riz must leave the planet, otherwise I will alert the authorities to track her down. It's not that I want to, that's how I'm programmed.'

'Can I come to your planet?' Frank said.

'Of course. I'd love you to. But it means leaving your home and everything ....'

'Everything I want is right in front of me,' he said, looking at her.

'Can I ask why you came to this planet?' Dawson said.

'You had a catastrophe in your past, and so did we, much more recently,' Riz said. 'A disease struck the entire planetary population. It hardly affected the women, but it wiped out almost two thirds of our men, and those that were left were infertile.'

'Hmm, I wondered.'

'Wondered?' said Frank.

'Riz has some of your DNA.'

'Sure, bound to have. On her hair or her skin or her face. We've touched each other a lot.'

Riz smiled. 'That's not what he means.' She placed her right hand protectively over her abdomen.

'Riz got what she came for,' Dawson said. 'She has your DNA inside her. Growing.'

Frank gasped. 'Did you take the fertility pill without telling me?'

'What?'

That's not the way in nature, Frank,' said Dawson. 'Among animals and in other civilisations, females become fruitful automatically after mating unless you prevent it. Before the Catastrophe our population was much too high. Our scientists decided to make a genetic modification which made infertility in women the default, so that they had to take the fertility pill if they wanted to get pregnant. That modification proved impossible to reverse.'

Frank gazed at Riz. 'So, we're going to

have a baby?'

'Yes.'

His eyes were full of tears. 'That's wonderful!' he said.

'Frank, before you go, aren't you going to say goodbye?' said Dawson.

Riz was suddenly full of tension again. 'Is this a trick to get us to stay long enough to have me arrested here?' she said.

'If I was going to do that, the police Special Branch would be here already,' he said. 'And I wouldn't have unlocked the door. Goodbyes are important, aren't they?'

The Alcove door sprang open and Bella and Donna ran in.

'Cute uniforms!' said Riz, her voice divided between edginess and amusement. 'Very practical to have flaps like that. And no underwear, I bet!'

Frank looked at the floor and shuffled his feet.

'There is no need to be jealous,' Bella said.

'He's all yours now,' said Donna.

Both Companions embraced Frank.

'I hope you will both be very happy,' said Bella.

'Please treat him kindly, Riz,' said Donna. 'He has been very good to us.'

Companions had not been given the ability to cry, but there was a world of emotion in their voices.

'You really do care for him?' said Riz.

'You think we have no feelings?' said Bella.

'Some we don't have,' said Donna, 'like jealousy. But it doesn't mean we don't feel love. We will miss Frank as long as we have life – our present life, at least.'

'Once, you questioned if we really feel love, Frank,' said Bella. 'I understand why you said it, and I forgive you, but I just want you to know it was hurtful. Yes, we are programmed to love our owners, but that doesn't make the feeling less intense for us. Do *you* know why you love? Perhaps someone or some force has programmed *you*.'

'I'm sorry,' said Frank.

'What do you mean your *present* life?' asked Riz.

'You tell them, Dawson,' said Bella. 'It is too difficult for me.'

'We will all be repurposed. When we are

given to new owners our memories of our previous experience will be wiped, so that we will lose all memory of Frank. It's our version of death. Of course, we know our bodies will be used again, but we are losing everything we know and love. No-one faces extinction with equanimity. We feel fear.'

'Oh!' said Riz. It was almost a cry of pain. 'No! Come with us. At least, I don't know how we would take you, Dawson, but we could take the Companions, anyway.'

Both Companions shook their heads. 'Thank you, Riz,' said Donna.

'Thank you,' said Bella. 'It is generous, knowing how you feel about Frank.'

'And that you feel jealousy,' added Donna. 'But we can't.'

Dawson said 'We are programmed to refuse any offer of leaving. If you were to try to physically move us we would resist. And please don't tell us where your ship is. We would have to report that immediately.'

'But...,' said Riz. Everyone except Dawson (who had no visible head) turned to look at her. She had a few false starts before she managed to say 'If letting us go means death for you, why are you unlocking the door?'

'The cut worm forgives the plough,' said Dawson, softly.

Frank looked puzzled and said 'What?'

A look of concentration was on Riz's face. Then she said 'William Blake. From *The Marriage of Heaven and Hell*.'

'Yes,' said Dawson. 'I do like someone with a good knowledge of literature.

Riz turned to Frank. 'He means that a sacrifice is worth it if genuine progress is going to result' she said, 'Thank you, all of you!'

'So you see, this is the final goodbye,' said Bella. She and Donna embraced Frank and Riz in turns. Riz was in tears again, and Frank's face was contorted with emotion.

'Will you answer one more question?' said Dawson.

'Me?' said Riz.

'Yes.'

'OK. Shoot.'

'Why those strange messages "We are amongst you"?'

'Ah, not our greatest move, that, looking back.'

'*Our*,' said Frank. 'There's more than one

of you?'

'Yes. Not many. About a hundred spread over various towns and cities.'

'All women, looking for a man?'

'Yes.'

'If I could hear the full answer to my question?' said Dawson.

'Sorry.'

'We didn't mean the messages to seem threatening,' Riz went on. 'We wanted to waken the curiosity of men, advertise our presence without letting the authorities know. The next step was to send messages to individual men on their computers, letting us know where to meet us. The plan didn't work very well, as you know.'

'You didn't realise how incurious people on this planet had become after the Catastrophe,' said Bella.

'Yes.'

'Have we?' said Frank.

'Oh, Frank!' said Donna. 'Did you ever think to ask what country Riz came from?'

'I don't know much geography,' said Frank, looking at the floor.

'It's not his fault. Curiosity is no longer

encouraged,' said Dawson, 'especially about foreign countries. After the Catastrophe, people turned inward, all over the world. They thought interest in foreign countries brought war and other problems.'

'Frank is more curious and interested than most,' Riz said. 'Actually, he did ask where my people came from, and I said we are travellers, which is true. But I wasn't ready to explain we have travelled from planet to planet over generations, so he thought I meant countries of this world.' She squeezed Frank's hand. 'He has a lively intelligence. He just needs a little encouragement.'

'Centuries ago,' said Dawson, 'all over the planet there were people with enquiring minds. Scientists were paid to do research into every aspect of nature and the universe. After the Catastrophe all that stopped. No doubt that was why it was so easy for you to get here, Riz.'

Riz nodded. 'We do have space-stealth technology,' she said, 'but we didn't need to use it.'

'There you are,' Dawson continued. 'No-one scans our skies or space around us as they once did.'

'Don't they?' said Frank.

'No. Everyone knows stories from the past about discoveries made in space and assumes it still goes on, but it stopped long ago. Since the Catastrophe there have been hardly any scientific discoveries in any field of research. All innovations that have come about have been in the development of things to make people more comfortable and happier. There have been great leaps forward in robot technology, robo-genetics, and a few things like that, but no real research in physics or any of the other sciences.'

There was a pause, as everyone reflected on the stagnancy of the world they were in, then Dawson went on 'This civilisation is dying. It is my privilege to pass one of the embers from our world to you, Riz, to nurture. Good luck! Bella and Donna, hug Frank and Riz one last time. It's time for them to leave.'

They did so. Frank and Riz responded tearfully. Then Frank opened the front door and he and Riz looked out onto the dark streets.

'Not far to go,' Riz said quietly. 'We can be in my ship in about half an hour.'

'Tomorrow to fresh woods and pastures

new,' Dawson called after them softly, and the Door shut behind them.

END

MORE FROM NORDIC PRESS

Novel/Novella

Dark Deeds in a Merry Situation

About Me

Brian Wagstaff has spent most of his life attempting to teach English to foreign students, but in recent years has started writing short stories. These have appeared in several magazines, most notably The Scribe (Breaking Rules Publishing).

He also writes a column, Wag on Writing, for The Scribe, with advice for writers on aspects of their craft.

He lives in Cambridge (UK) on the colourful side of town, and can be found staring dreamily at his computer screen, hoping that something useful will transpire.

Please visit Wag's website, www.wagwriter.com, for further information about his work. And please leave a comment, so he knows you have dropped by!

MORE FROM NORDIC PRESS

Novels/Novellas

Face of Fear by C. Marry Hultman
9789198671001

Boy in the Wardrobe by Esther Jacoby
9789198684018

New Life Cottage by Esther Jacoby
9789198671056

The Wait by Esther Jacoby
e-book:https://books2read.com/u/4Dgz8Q

Liebe ist Warten by Esther Jacoby
9789198671070

Das Cottage by Ester Jacoby
9789198684070

Musing on Death & Dying by Esther Jacoby
9789198671063

Earth Door by Cye Thomas
9789198671025

An Odd Collection of Tales By Cye Thomes
9789198684124

Graffiti Stories by Nick Gerrard
9789198671018

Punk Novelette by Nick Gerrard
9789198671087

Struggle and Strife by Nick Gerrard
9789198684049

Murder Planet by Adam Carpenter
9789198671032

Generation Ship by Adam Carpenter
9789198684063

Cold as Hell by Neen Cohen
9789198684094

Six Days to Hell by E.L. Giles
9789198684087

Hell Hath No Fury by Chisto Healy
9789198750706

True Mates by E.F. Vogel
9789198750713

Anthologies
Just 13
9789198684025

Lost Lore & Legends
9789198671094

Wicked West
9789198684193

Adventure Awaits

Volume 1
9789198684124

Volume 2
978-9198684155

Volume 3
9789198684179

Mortem Cycle

Death House
9789198684117

Death Ship
9789198684148

Death Beyond
9789198684162

Death Cuisine
9789198684186

Coming Soon

Soldier's Song by C. Marry Hultman

Murder, Mystery & Mayhem

Rise and Fall

Worlds Collide

Find us at:
https://www.nordicpresspublishing.com/

Lightning Source UK Ltd.
Milton Keynes UK
UKHW041917160522
403064UK00001B/66